Keeping Score

Linda Sue Park

CLARION BOOKS
NEW YORK

Clarion Books
a Houghton Mifflin Company imprint
215 Park Avenue South, New York, NY 10003
Copyright © 2008 by Linda Sue Park

Book design by Michelle Gengaro-Kokmen.
The text was set in 12-point Warnock Pro.

www.clarionbooks.com

Printed in the U.S.A.

Full cataloging information is available from the Library of Congress.

ISBN: 978-0-618-92799-9
LC number: 2007046522

QUM   10 9 8 7 6 5 4 3 2 1

To Nancy Quade,
with thanks for all those Opening Days

Contents

One

THE NEW GUY

Brooklyn, N.Y.
July 1951

"*H*ow's come you guys don't bunt?"

Maggie was sitting on the stoop. On the sidewalk in front of their house, Joey-Mick finished tying his shoe with a double knot. He shrugged but didn't answer.

Then he picked up his glove and glared at it. He tightened the worn leather lace that was always coming undone, and prodded the hole in the top of one of the fingers. The glove was a hand-me-down from their uncle Leo, and the only reason it was still in one piece, Maggie thought, was because it didn't want to face her brother's wrath if it fell apart.

"They bunt all the time in the majors," Maggie said. "Well, not all the time, but when they need to. Nobody on your team bunts, hardly never. Don't they teach you how?"

"We *know* how," Joey-Mick said as he started plunking a ball into the pocket of the glove, *thunk— thunk—thunk*. "But it's lots more important to get good at hitting." He stopped plunking long enough to tug at the bill of his cap; Maggie thought that the cap over his new crewcut made him look like he didn't have any hair at all. "If you played, you wouldn't hafta ask that."

Maggie pressed her lips together hard. Whenever she tried to talk baseball with Joey-Mick, he always used that older-so-I-know-way-more-than-you voice and said she didn't or wouldn't or couldn't understand because she didn't play ball herself.

It wasn't fair. She was nine-going-on-ten, and she knew plenty about baseball, and way more about the Dodgers than he did. Unless she was in school, she never missed a game on the radio. Joey-Mick might go out to play with his friends during a broadcast, but not Maggie.

Like today. The Dodgers' game would be starting soon, in Pittsburgh against the Pirates, and here was Joey-Mick waiting for his friend Davey, so they could go to the park to have a catch.

Maggie stood up. She was leaving as well, to walk the two blocks to the firehouse and listen to the radio with the guys.

"Gotta go," she said. "Us *real* fans have a game to listen to."

New York was the only city in the whole country with three baseball teams. The Yankees of the American League were the winningest team in all of baseball. They had been World Series champions a whopping *thirteen* times. And the National League Giants had won the World Series four times in their history.

The Brooklyn Dodgers, who were in the National League with the Giants, had *never* won the World Series.

Not ever.

Not even once.

It was what Maggie wanted more than anything in the world: for the Dodgers to win the World Series. It seemed like she had wanted it ever since she was born. Every year the Dodgers—whose nickname to Brooklynites was "Dem Bums"—came close, either winning the National League pennant or finishing in the top three. But the biggest prize, the World Series championship, always seemed to slip away from them.

Although Maggie knew it wasn't true, she felt as if the first words she had learned when she was a baby were "Wait till next year!"—the unofficial official slogan of Dodger fans.

Charcoal, the mostly black firehouse dog, always knew when Maggie was coming, and she knew he knew, so even before she saw him, she took from her pocket a folded paper napkin that held a half-slice of salami. When he bounded down the street to meet her, she was ready.

She held out the salami, which he snapped down without chewing.

"Charky! Where are your manners?" she said, shaking her head and smiling at the same time.

The dog led the way to the firehouse, where the guys were sitting out front on folding chairs, boots and suspenders and toothpicks, with the radio already tuned to the game. As soon as George caught sight of her, he jumped to his feet and went and got another chair. After greetings, they all settled in to listen, Charky flopping down at Maggie's feet. A routine, but one she never got tired of.

The call came in at a crucial moment: The Dodgers had just tied the game.

"Shouldn't be long, Maggie-o," George said as he opened the door on the driver's side of the fire engine and waited while Charky bounded onto the seat. "Doesn't sound like anything serious. You better get that lead and keep it for us."

"I will," Maggie promised, stepping to the side of the bay to get out of the way. "Stay cool," she called out as George hopped into the engine's cab.

Whenever Dad left the house to go to work, Maggie and Joey-Mick always told him to "stay cool." It came from something he often said to them: "When things get hot, you gotta stay cool."

During Dad's firehouse days, Maggie would get sent home if an emergency call came in. But now she didn't have to leave when the guys went out on a job.

"You're in charge," George had said the first time she stayed. Which had made her feel quite important.

She watched until the engine was out of sight, then walked over to the radio at the side of the bay and turned up the volume so she could listen while she worked.

George was very strict about keeping the firehouse tidy. He had learned it from Maggie's dad, how keeping the whole place neat and organized could save precious time in an emergency. Most days at the firehouse when there weren't any calls, the guys spent a lot of time cleaning. Today Maggie planned to surprise them by sweeping up while they were out.

Dad had been a fireman at this station until three years ago. One afternoon when Maggie was six, Mom answered a knock at the door. Two cops were on the stoop. There had been a fire, and Dad was hurt. They didn't know how bad.

Maggie could still remember every detail of the ride to the hospital, the dome light flashing and the siren shrieking and Mom holding her hand tight enough that it hurt. They saw Dad for a few moments before the operation to fix his leg, his face so black with soot that you couldn't tell where the soot ended and his hair and mustache began, and when he smiled at them, his teeth looked the whitest they had ever been—smiled even though the pain must have been too awful to imagine. And he said, "You weren't none of yous worried, were ya?"

Maggie had seen the tears tracking down her mother's face as she cleared her throat and answered, "Pish, I couldn't be bothered. I was getting the dinner, and it'll be gone cold now, thank you very much."

They were clustered around his hospital bed when he woke up from the operation. "Everybody staying cool?" he asked groggily, the first words out of his mouth.

Later he told them a little more about what had happened. "I went crashin' through the floor, right? And when I got my wits back, I got down low, where the air was a little better, and I started crawling. Every inch I crawled I tried to think about something cool. Maggie eating ice cream, Joey-Mick hosing down the wagon, your mom at Jones Beach when we were courting—"

"What's so cool about that?" Joey-Mick asked.

Dad winked. "—in her bathing suit—"

"Joseph!" Maggie's mom put one hand to her mouth, half annoyed and half laughing.

"Can't help it, Rosie, it's the truth."

And staying cool had helped Dad save his own life, and maybe George's and Vince's too, for even with a shattered leg he managed to crawl as far as the door, where the other guys found him and dragged him out just as the whole roof collapsed. If he hadn't made it to the door on his own, all three of them might have died inside.

"Some guys would hate it," George had said to Maggie when Dad was reassigned to a desk job. "They couldn't stand bein' in an office, they'd sorta dry up and—and shrivel away. But not your pop. 'Cause he loves the department, see. Really loves it."

Maggie knew without asking that Mom was glad not to have to worry about Dad on the job anymore. But she also knew that he missed being at the firehouse. It was one of the reasons she still went there.

"Told ya," George said to Terry. "Told ya she'd get the lead for us."

The guys were back. As George had predicted, the call had been an easy one, nothing but smolder by the time they got there. Garbage in an alley had caught fire from a carelessly tossed cigarette butt. The owner of the shop next to the alley had telephoned for help first, and then gone out with a bucket of water and doused the fire himself. The guys had helped clean up the alley and cautioned the shop owner not to let trash pile up like that again.

Maggie made a tiny gesture that no one else could see, moving her forefinger against her thumb in the sign of the cross. She always did that when the guys came back safely.

George took off his helmet. He ran his hand over his head the way he often did; the other guys always said he was making sure he still had some hair left. It might have been true, but Maggie liked how his hair receded in a curve; it looked like a smile.

"Terry said we were gonna lose the game," George said. "He said sure, we got it tied up, but that would be it for us, and the Pirates would come back and score."

"Hey, it was a good guess," Terry said. "Happened *twice* in the past week." Blond and stocky, he stood in front of Maggie so she could snap his suspender straps against his ample belly. She didn't remember how this ritual had gotten started, but she had been snapping his straps for ages now. Whenever he got back from a call.

"Yeah, but you know what *I* said," George answered. "I said, we left Maggie-o in charge, she's gonna take care of everything. And look"—he waved his arm broadly—"she got the place swept up, too!"

"So what happened?" Terry asked eagerly. "How'd they do it?"

Maggie explained: how Brooklyn had scored three runs in the top of the sixth inning to go ahead, 7–4, and one more in the top of the ninth, and how the Pirates had been held scoreless the whole rest of the game.

"How many'd he strike out?" Terry asked. "He got six before we left—he get any more?"

Maggie knew who Terry was asking about: Preacher Roe, the pitcher.

"Yep," she said. "He got—"

She stopped, frowning. At least one more, she knew that for sure. But had there been another one? Or maybe even two? Or was she getting it mixed up with earlier in the game?

Terry waved away her hesitation. "'Sokay, Maggie-o. I can find out tomorrow."

"I think maybe two," Maggie said. "Anyway, he was pitching really good."

"Musta been, seeing how they didn't score any more."

The talk about the game continued until it became talk about the season and the team, other teams, other players, and especially, dreams of future glory, the way it always did.

On the walk home, Maggie went over the game again in her head. Why couldn't she remember how many strikeouts Preacher Roe had gotten? She knew he was Terry's favorite player; she should've been paying more attention. But no matter what Joey-Mick thought, she didn't believe that playing the game herself would make any difference, would help her remember any better.

The thing was, Maggie didn't want to play baseball. Not because it was a boy thing—it wasn't anymore. There had been a real league for women during the war, and Maggie's best friend, Treecie, had once said that if they had the chance, girls could do anything boys could do—"except pee standing up." Maggie had laughed in both shock and admiration. She couldn't even think of things like that, much less bring herself to say them.

To Maggie, being a fan was a whole separate thing from playing the game yourself. Joey-Mick might be able to tell you that Carl Furillo's batting average was around .300 and that Don Newcombe had won most of his games so far. But Maggie had it down cold: Furillo was batting .304, and the Newk had six wins.

It was like the movies. You could go to the pictures every week, know all about the stars, read everything in the magazines—and still not want to be an actress yourself. Their mother, Rose, was like that. She had told Maggie that when she first came to New York from Ireland, she went to the pictures every chance she got, "sometimes three or four in a week!"

Mom was kind of solid around her middle now, with a few streaks of gray in her hair that Dad sometimes teased her about—his own hair being jet black—but her eyes were as blue as a calm sky, and her skin so clear that her face always looked like she had just washed it. Maggie could imagine a much younger Rose getting dressed up and going out for a good time.

Baseball and the Dodgers were even bigger than the movies. You had to go to the movie theater to see a picture, but the radio, with announcer Red Barber, brought the Bums right into Maggie's home. Into her street, too, so Maggie didn't mind running errands during a game. She would walk past the row of houses that looked just like hers, all built of dull brownish yellow brick, one window downstairs two windows up—to Pinky the butcher or Mr. and Mrs. Floyd at the bakery or the drugstore, and she wouldn't miss a single pitch. Everyone would have their radios on, the sound of the game trailing in and out of each doorway like a long thread that tied the whole neighborhood together.

The thread almost always led Maggie to the firehouse, her second home. When she and Joey-Mick were younger, they would stop by often to visit Dad. He would give them little jobs to do. And with all the guys there, it was like having a bunch of favorite uncles to joke around with anytime you wanted. They had spoiled her with piggyback rides and Hershey bars, and George always gave her a bite of his sandwich, so that over the years, Maggie had developed a ferocious love for horseradish.

He would hold out the sandwich; she would lean over and bite into it. Sometimes it was messy, like the time her bite dislodged a whole slice of tomato and it sort of dangled from her mouth until she managed to wolf it down. Once she even pulled out all the ham, leaving behind two empty pieces of bread. George had pretended to be mad at her; she was only six then, and for a few moments she had been scared that he really *was* mad—until he laughed.

But best of all were the Dodgers' games. Listening to them and talking to the guys about baseball, it never mattered one bit that she was a girl who didn't play ball herself.

A few days after the game against the Pirates, Maggie headed for the firehouse again. As she drew near, she cocked her head a little. She could hear the radio as usual, but Red Barber's voice was being drowned out by the sound of boos and jeering. What was going on? Had Philadelphia scored? That couldn't be—it was Brooklyn's turn to bat. . . .

Terry and Vince and George were up out of their chairs, booing and hissing and jostling a fourth man, someone she didn't know.

"New guy?" Maggie murmured to Charky, who had loped out to meet her.

"Hey, Maggie-o!" George called out. "You're just in time. You're not gonna believe this—" He pointed in a big exaggerated motion at the new guy.

Maggie saw that the new guy was built like her dad. Maybe not big all over the way her dad was, but tall and not skinny—lots of muscles. A flattop haircut. Dressed like the rest of them, in blue. Younger than George, nice brown eyes.

Then Maggie saw what George was *really* pointing at: the radio at the new guy's feet. Not the firehouse's usual radio, which sat where it always did, at one side of the bay doors, but a smaller, newer one.

"What's he need another—" Maggie started to ask, but the two radios themselves answered her. Red Barber's voice was all mixed up with someone else's— a different voice, coming from the second radio.

Maggie stared at the radio for a moment, just to be sure. Then she looked at George because she couldn't quite bring herself to look at the new guy.

"That's right, Mags. A *Giants* fan!" George jeered.

"All right, all right," New Guy said. "I'll turn it down, see?" He turned a black knob on his radio. The words of Russ Hodges, the radio voice of the New York Giants, faded away, and Maggie could hear Red again, declaring Don Newcombe out on a slow roller to first.

Then the new guy lay down right there on the pavement, on his back with his head next to his radio. He put his hands behind his head and grinned up at George. "I can hear just fine, but it won't mess up *your* game, see?"

George slapped one hand against the other in disgust. "That's not the point, Junior. There's never been a Giants fan in this house—this here is a *Bums* house."

"George . . ." Maggie hesitated, not wanting to contradict him. "My dad—"

"Yeah, yeah, your dad's a Yankee fan. But at least they're not in the National League," George said. "And besides, he's not at this house no more, so—"

He stopped and glanced at Maggie quickly, and she knew he was thinking about Dad's accident, maybe wondering if the reminder would bother her. She bobbed her head at him; it was okay because Dad was okay.

New Guy raised himself up on one elbow and looked at Maggie. "You Joe's kid?" he asked. "Teeny Joe?"

Maggie nodded, wondering. Dad's name was Joe Fortini. There were a lot of Joes around, so ages ago he'd gotten the nickname "Teeny Joe," which was funny because he was a big guy with a big voice and a big mustache and nothing about him was teeny. Only his good friends called him Teeny Joe.

The new guy sat up and extended his hand. "Pleased to meet you, miss."

Maggie shook his hand. "Who are you?" Probably sounded rude, but curiosity won out over manners. "And how come you know my dad?"

"Got me the job, didn't he," he said. "Name's Jim Maine."

So that was it. Dad interviewed guys who wanted to be firemen. He talked about his work a lot; he was proud of picking out the ones who would stick, who would make it through the training and then do good on the job, and he called them his boys.

"Hello, Mr. Maine," she said politely.

Jim grinned up at her. "Jim'll do," he said. "And if you're Maggie-o, then it's true about your name."

Maggie blushed. Dad must have told him. It was odd to think that they had talked about her.

Her father had grown up in the Bronx, just a few blocks away from Yankee Stadium, a Yanks fan from the guts out. When Maggie's brother was born, he was named Joseph Michael—Joseph for his dad, sure, but also for Joe DiMaggio.

Maggie had heard Dad tell the story a hundred times. "And when a girl come along two years later, I knew just what I was gonna call her," he would say whenever the subject came up. "Maggie-o! Don't matter that they're not exactly the same. DiMaggio . . . Maggie-o, get it?"

But Maggie's mother had refused to let him put "Maggie-o" on the birth certificate. It read "Margaret Olivia." Maggie's great-grandmother in Ireland had been a Margaret, and Olivia de Havilland was Mom's favorite actress; *Gone with the Wind* had come out two years before Maggie was born, with Miss de Havilland playing that nice girl Melanie, and "if Scarlett had been more like Melanie, there wouldn't have been nearly the trouble, so you're Margaret Olivia after your great-grandmother and Olivia de Havilland, never mind what your father says" was how Mom always finished the story.

Now Jim put his hands back behind his head and chuckled. "Good ol' Teeny Joe," he said. "Your old man's really something, y'know? Even if you don't like the Yankees, you gotta give him credit. Naming *both* your kids after your favorite player—that's class."

Maggie tilted her head and half shrugged, half smiled. She was pretty sure she liked this new guy.

"So how's come you're not a Yankee fan like your dad?" Jim asked.

Maggie frowned. The idea that she could be a fan of any team other than the Dodgers! But it wasn't a dumb question. The Yankees' and Giants' fans in her neighborhood were, as Mom might say, as rare as peaches in winter, but they were usually whole families following the same team.

"Dunno," she said. "Guess it's 'cause I was born here. I mean, I knew my dad was a Yankee fan, but me and my brother, we always listened to the Dodgers' games."

"Yeah, and you know what else?" George growled. "Teeny Joe *never* listened to the Yanks here. Nosirree, he knew we were a Dodger house and we—we respected him for respectin' that. Not like *some*."

And George ran his hand over his head and turned away. Jim and Maggie grinned at each other behind his back.

"Gotta go," Maggie said.

"Be seeing you," Jim said.

And she heard the last out of the game while she was in Mr. Aldo's shop getting a box of sugar for Mom. 2–0, a close one, but the Dodgers won, and Maggie skipped home.

Two

1—PITCHER

*T*he phone rang early the next morning. It was Treecie.

Maggie and Treecie were best-friends-for-life, sworn way back in second grade. Not a blood vow— they had both been too scared to prick their fingers with a pin—but a spit vow, which everyone knew was almost as good.

Treecie's whole name was Mary Theresa Brady. Her mother was Mary, too, so Mary Theresa was called Theresa, which had gotten shortened to Treecie. She was shorter than Maggie, but they both had brown hair and blue eyes and freckles. Treecie had more freckles than Maggie—they had once tried and failed to count them, but you could tell just by looking. Maggie got tan in the summer, like her dad. Treecie freckled.

Their birthdays were exactly one month apart— November 19 for Treecie, December 19 for Maggie. They had already chosen their confirmation names:

Treecie was going to be Mary Theresa Margaret Brady, and Maggie would be Margaret Olivia Theresa Fortini. Even though they wouldn't be confirmed until they were thirteen, it was nice to have it planned out.

Treecie wanted to be a photographer. Last year, when they turned nine, Treecie had gotten her first camera, a used Brownie. Ever since then, Maggie had spent a lot of time posing for Treecie. Inside, outside, portraits, action shots, candids. . . . Film and developing were expensive, so Treecie didn't actually *take* very many photos, but she had Maggie pose all the same. "It's good practice," Treecie would insist as she peered through the viewfinder. "I have to develop my eye."

Treecie was calling to say that she wanted to take photos of Maggie "with nature stuff." In Brooklyn that meant the park, and half an hour later, Maggie stepped out onto her front stoop just as Treecie came into sight from around the corner.

"We should have brought Charky," Maggie said as they passed between the concrete pillars that marked the park's entrance. "He loves the park."

The entrance they used was diagonally across the street from Maggie's house. The girls were allowed to go to the park on their own so long as they stayed within calling distance of the pillars.

"Not this time," Treecie said firmly. "I got stuff I wanna do; he'd just get in the way." She looked around. "There," she said, "that little tree."

Maggie walked over to the tree and turned to face Treecie.

"No, not like that. I want you to stand farther back and put your head in between the branches. So there's leaves all around you."

Maggie ducked under the lowest branch to get behind it, but straightened up too quickly.

"Ouch!" she said, rubbing her head. "Never mind, I'm okay." She parted the leafy twigs, trying to find a place to pose comfortably. "Yeesh, scratchy."

Leaves were tickling the back of her neck—at least she hoped they were leaves. What if they were bugs? She brushed at her neck with her hand just in case.

At last she turned her face toward Treecie. "Hey!" she said.

Treecie was standing a few yards away. She had made a square using her thumbs and forefingers; with one eye closed and her hands in front of her face, she peered at Maggie through the square.

"You don't have your camera with you?" Maggie said. "First you wanna take pictures of me without any film, and now without a *camera* even?"

"It's called 'framing the shot,'" Treecie said. "I'm learning how to frame a shot. I don't need the camera for that."

"*I* do!" Maggie protested. "I mean, *I* don't need a camera, but I need *you* to have one! I look like an idiot standing here and—and posing—and no camera. . . ."

Treecie lowered her hands from her face. "You're a photographer's model," she said earnestly. "It doesn't matter what *you* look like—it's *the shot* that matters."

"So you're saying that I *do* look like an idiot?"

Treecie put her hands on her hips. "No, I did not

say that. Did you hear me say that? Did you hear me say, 'Maggie Fortini, you look like an idiot'?"

Maggie laughed; she couldn't help it. Treecie looked relieved that Maggie wasn't mad anymore. "I won't make you stay there for long, promise," Treecie said. She put the "square" up to her face again, and with a sigh, Maggie went back to posing.

The results: Zero photos, but one bruise on her head, one scratch under her chin, and one mosquito bite.

Not that she was counting.

Treecie was lucky, Maggie thought, to be so sure about what she wanted to be when she grew up. Maggie didn't know yet, and she worried about it. She tried on different ideas. Working in a shop, maybe. "Because you get to meet people, and I could listen to the games while I'm working," Maggie explained.

"But you'd never get to see anything new," Treecie objected. "Just the same stuff every day. That would get boring."

Another time Maggie had proposed becoming a nurse. Treecie's mom was a nurse, and so was Maggie's aunt Maria in Canada. Treecie had replied, "No. Not a nurse. A doctor. Wait, I know—a surgeon. And I'll take pictures of your operations."

"Maybe," Maggie said. It sounded kind of gruesome, but Treecie's ideas were always interesting, that was for sure.

Both of Treecie's parents worked, which meant that every year when school ended, she and her two younger sisters went to Long Island for the summer, to stay on the farm owned by their uncle. Maggie had spent a wonderful week there two years ago, the only time she had ever been away from home on her own.

A few days after the photo session in the park, Treecie left for Long Island. Maggie was used to it now, the summers without Treecie, but being used to it didn't mean she *liked* it. She always missed Treecie terribly, especially during the first couple of weeks. Sometimes Maggie played with other kids on the block: hopscotch, jumping rope, the playgrounds in Prospect Park during the day, and after supper a regular game of kick the can. But when Treecie was away, Maggie's best friends were the radio and the guys at the firehouse.

And Charky. Of course.

It was so hot that a ragged band of sweat was already darkening Joey-Mick's cap as he left the house for baseball practice. Every inch of Maggie's clothes seemed stuck to her. The Dodgers had a day off, and the July afternoon would feel even longer and hotter without a game to listen to. Maggie knew that the players needed their rest, but she was counting the hours until the game started tomorrow.

Joey-Mick was in his first season in a real league. Not stickball on the street but games on the diamonds in Prospect Park—a regular schedule, a manager, an umpire. Just like in the major leagues.

Uniforms, too. When Joey-Mick first put his on, Maggie thought it looked like pajamas, all baggy in the shirt and floppy in the legs. But then she saw the rest of the team at their first game, and Joey-Mick's uniform fit better than almost anyone else's. He was one of the tallest boys on the team.

Joey-Mick played second base, same as his favorite player, Jackie Robinson. And if he got to first when he was at bat, he would move around on the base path—hopping, prancing, faking a steal—just like Jackie.

Last season, when Maggie first started listening to the Dodger broadcasts—*really* listening to them, paying attention, learning the game—she decided that Jackie Robinson was her favorite player, too.

Not because she was a copycat. Or because he was the first-ever Negro in the league, which everyone knew was a big deal. So big that even though Dad was a Yankees fan, he was a Jackie Robinson fan, too. "Biggest thing that's ever happened in baseball" was how Dad put it.

But Maggie had been only five years old when Jackie broke in, and she hadn't understood very much about baseball back then. So she didn't have any real memories of his first year with the Dodgers. And now, four years later, almost every team had Negro ballplayers.

No, it was the *spark* Jackie had, how he seemed to light up the whole game when he was on the field. So she told Joey-Mick that Jackie was her favorite player, too.

"No dice," Joey-Mick said immediately.

"Why not?"

"'Cause he's *my* favorite player. We can't both have

him as our favorite player, and I had him first. So you gotta pick someone else."

"But why can't both of us—"

"Because," he said firmly. "Now, who's your second-favorite player?"

Maggie hesitated. She still wanted Jackie, but it was an interesting question. "Pee Wee," she said. "No, wait. Roy Campanella."

"See, there you go. One of them's can be your favorite player."

She had chosen Campy in the end, which was no shame—he was terrific, both at the plate and behind it. But she didn't feel the same way about Campy that she did about Jackie. She wondered why she hadn't fought harder. Joey-Mick wasn't in charge of the world. Since when did he get to decide favorite-player rules? But if she had stuck with Jackie, her brother would think she was copycatting, no matter what she said.

Joey-Mick slammed the door on his way out. Maggie sighed and tugged at the collar of her dress so she could blow down the front of it. Then she wandered into the kitchen, opened the Frigidaire door, and took out a bottle of milk. Not to drink, but so she could press the cool glass against her forehead.

"Put that back," Mom said automatically without even looking up from the onion she was chopping. "And I'll go to my grave telling you to keep the Frigidaire door closed!"

Maggie put the bottle back on the shelf. She let the

door swing shut and made sure to stand right where she could feel the last puff of lovely cool air.

"What's for supper?" she asked, more out of boredom than curiosity.

"Sausage and macaroni," Mom answered. "It's Wednesday, so it is."

Monday, Wednesday, and Friday were macaroni nights. Tuesday, Thursday, and Saturday meant potatoes. Sundays alternated. That was how it had been ever since Maggie's parents got married—Rose Fitzpatrick and Joe Fortini, Irish and Italian. The only time the pattern was interrupted was when one of the uncles came for dinner. If it was Uncle Pat, Mom cooked potatoes no matter what day it was; for Uncle Leo, macaroni. Maggie liked both potatoes and macaroni, and she was glad she didn't have to eat just one all the time. At Treecie's house they almost always had potatoes.

Mom nodded toward a plate on the countertop. "There," she said, "for that dog friend of yours." And she pointed the tip of her knife at the naked bone that had already done double-duty in Sunday's roast and Monday's soup.

Maggie gave Mom a hug. "Thanks," she said.

"Oof. Don't be hanging on to me in this heat. Go on with yourself now."

Maggie smiled as she took the bone and left. Mom wouldn't have a dog in the house, but a week never went by that she didn't have a little something for Maggie to give Charky.

The dog greeted her as usual, half a block from the

firehouse. Maggie made him sit, beg, and speak before she gave him the bone. He hurried back to the station, looking over his shoulder as he loped along, to make sure she was following.

When Maggie got near the firehouse, she could see the new guy—Jim, she reminded herself, Jim Maine—sitting out front with his radio. The Giants' game. Nobody else was around; the other guys were probably inside.

Jim had a notebook on his lap and was writing in it. He didn't look up when Charky bounded past and went to his bed, where he lay down, gnawing joyfully.

Jim seemed very busy with whatever he was working on. It would probably be rude to interrupt him. Maggie turned to leave.

"... and Mays rounds third—he's going to try to score! The throw comes in—he slides—the ump . . . SAFE! HE'S SAFE! He's in under the tag! Mays has just scored from first base on a single! Howdya like that!?"

Jim let out a whoop and raised his arms in celebration. That was when he saw Maggie.

"Hey there!" he said.

"Hi. I just—I brought a bone for Charky."

Jim turned around to look at the dog and grinned. "Lucky dog," he said. "Say, did you hear that last play? Wasn't that something?"

Maggie nodded.

Jim shook his head, still smiling. "It's gonna seem like a mistake," he said. "Later, if anyone sees this, they're gonna think I left out a play—a throwing error or something." As he scribbled in the notebook, his voice lowered, so he seemed to be talking to himself, but Maggie could still hear what he was saying. "Scoring from first on a single . . . drew the throw too, so now they got a runner on second."

Maggie took a step closer and tilted her head so she could read sort of sideways rather than upside-down. There was writing on both pages of the open spread, and a lot of little squares filled with tiny numbers and letters and lines. In a column on the left side of each page, Jim had written the names of the players—the Cubs on one page, the Giants on the other.

"What's that you're doing?" Maggie asked.

"You never seen anyone keep score before?"

She shook her head. "What do the numbers mean?"

His eyebrows went up. "It's kinda complicated," he said. "I dunno—oh, hold up a minute."

The next batter hit a hard liner caught by the shortstop, who then beat the baserunner back to second: Unassisted double play to end the inning.

Jim shook his head. "Great play," he said ruefully as he wrote something down. "Okay, where was I? The numbers. Well, for a start, you gotta know the game pretty good."

Maggie stuck out her chin. "I know the game just fine."

Jim stared at her for a moment, then grinned. "Wouldn't doubt it, you being Teeny Joe's kid. Even seeing you're a girl. But lemme see you prove it."

"How?"

"Well . . . okay. What was so special about that scoring play just now?"

Maggie shrugged. "Nobody hardly ever scores from first base on a single," she said, with a bored little drone in her voice, as though she was reciting a lesson at school. Who did this guy think he was, quizzing her on baseball? "Depending on where it's hit, you usually only get to second, but if it's hit to right field and you got good speed, you could maybe get to third, but if the right fielder has a strong arm it'll prob'ly be a close play, so for him to make it all the way home—he musta had a big jump on the pitch, or maybe the hit-and-run was on, and then—"

Jim held up his hands, laughing. "Okay, okay! Wow, you oughta be on the radio your own self! The thing is, keeping score, you gotta be more than just a fan. . . ."

His voiced trailed off. He was looking at her hard, his head tilted and his eyes narrowed, but there seemed to be a twinkle there, too. Maggie looked right back at him and kept her chin high, but inside she squirmed a little. It was like he was trying to see right inside her brain.

Jim seemed to make up his mind. He handed her the notebook and pencil, then went inside the bay doors to fetch another folding chair, which he set up next to his own.

"Sit," he said. "Easiest way is if you watch while I do it. If you're really interested, you'll pick it up on your own, most of it anyhow, and I'll explain the rest."

By the end of the game, Maggie knew how the defense was numbered. Not their uniform numbers, but their *position* numbers. Jim tore a sheet out of the back of the notebook so she could write it down to study at home.

1 – pitcher
2 – catcher
3 – first base
4 – second base
5 – third base
6 – shortstop
7 – left field
8 – center field
9 – right field

Jim also showed her what the numbers in the little squares meant. They told what each batter had done. "4-3" written in the square opposite the batter's name meant that a ground ball had been hit to the second baseman (4) who had thrown it to the first baseman (3) for the out.

Jim could look at his score sheet and see exactly what had happened in any inning. Which was way better than just keeping it in your head, because when you were trying to remember what happened in a game, only the big exciting plays came to mind. But Maggie knew that baseball was often a game of little things—the pitcher falling behind in the count, the good throw to keep a runner from advancing, the slide to break up a double play—and those were hard to keep track of. Jim's score sheet didn't have every single thing written down, but the things that were there could really help you remember.

"Can I come again tomorrow?" she asked. "Will you show me some more?"

"Sure," Jim said. "Tomorrow's a night game. I'm off-duty, but I'll meet you here anyway. If your ma says it's okay."

Maggie let her eyes twinkle at him. "I'll ask my dad."

"Ha! Okay, Miss Maggie-o. And one other thing. Dodgers play tomorrow night too, but we'll be listening to the *Giants'* game—got it?"

"That's all right," Maggie said. She knew the Dodgers would be on the other radio; she could find out the score whenever she wanted. Then she frowned. "But that means we'll have to have your radio turned up, won't we? So we can both hear it? The other guys—"

"Hmm." Jim looked thoughtful. "Yeah. Well, I'll figure something out. You just worry about learning those position numbers, okay?"

Maggie trotted home after giving Charky a hug. She already knew that she wasn't going to tell Joey-Mick about learning how to score a game, not yet. Not until she could do a whole game all by herself. Maybe she would just sit there in front of the radio, writing stuff down, and when he asked what she was doing, *then* she would tell him.

She might even teach him, too. If he asked very nicely.

Jim had brought a long extension cord to the firehouse so they could put his radio on the sidewalk a good few yards away from the drive. George expressed both astonishment and disapproval over Maggie's listening to the Giants' games, but she assured him it was only so she could learn to keep score herself, "and then I'll be doing the Dodgers' games, okay, George?" He had given his grudging approval. Not that she needed it, but she didn't want him to be mad at her.

So much to learn about keeping score! Maggie was torn between wanting to know all of it *now* and the fun of discovering a new thing or two or three every day.

Jim showed Maggie how to list the batting order, each team on a separate page. Then you wrote the inning number, one through nine, across the top, and drew lines down the page to make narrow columns for each inning. Those vertical lines and the pale blue horizontal lines printed on the page formed boxes, each no bigger than her thumbnail.

When a player batted, you wrote the play down in the little box opposite his name, in the column for the correct inning. Special numbers and letters were used for different plays. For example, Jim taught her that "K" stood for strikeout. There were two ways for a player to strike out—by swinging and missing, or by *not* swinging at a pitch that was called a strike by the umpire. For a swing and a miss, you wrote a normal K. But for a called strike, you used a backward one: Ʞ.

It was a handy way to tell the difference, but more than that, Maggie loved how the backward K looked so strange on the page—askew and confused, just like a batter befuddled by a pitch.

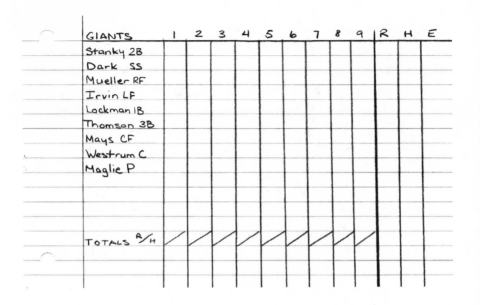

GIANTS	1	2	3	4	5	6	7	8	9	R	H	E
Stanky 2B												
Dark SS												
Mueller RF												
Irvin LF												
Lockman 1B												
Thomson 3B												
Mays CF												
Westrum C												
Maglie P												
TOTALS R/H												

"Strikeout looking is worse than strikeout swing-ing," Maggie declared. "At least swinging, you know the guy tried."

"Yeah," Jim agreed, "except when the ump makes a bum call—when it shoulda been a ball."

A strikeout was easy to record, just one letter. But for some plays, Maggie had to squeeze a lot more into the little square. Like "6-4-3" for a double play when a ground ball was hit to the shortstop, who threw to the second baseman, who threw to the first baseman.

It was often a pure aggravation trying to make it all fit. Good thing for Maggie that penmanship was one of her best subjects in school. She discovered that it helped to have a really sharp pencil, so she bought a nickel sharpener from Mr. Aldo at the corner store and carried it around in her pocket.

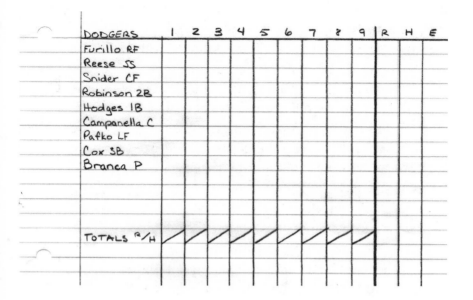

DODGERS	1	2	3	4	5	6	7	8	9	R	H	E
Furillo RF												
Reese SS												
Snider CF												
Robinson 2B												
Hodges 1B												
Campanella C												
Pafko LF												
Cox 3B												
Branca P												
TOTALS R/H												

The tiny numbers and letters looked like gibberish—WP, HBP, E6—unless you knew what they meant, which made scoring like a secret language. Or maybe it was like becoming a member of a special club, one that only the most serious baseball fans could join. Maggie learned fast; after only a week, she could score almost any play on her own. Now, whenever the guys were out on a call during a game, she could tell them exactly what had happened when they got back. She could tell Joey-Mick, too. Not just the score, or the big exciting plays, but the little things as well.

One afternoon as he was leaving the firehouse for the day, Jim asked Maggie to keep score of the Giants' game for him that evening. "I'm helping a buddy move house," he said, handing her his scorebook. "I'll probably get to hear a lot of the game, but I don't wanna miss anything. I wouldn't ask, 'cept I know that the Dodgers aren't playing tonight."

Never had Maggie kept score so carefully. By the end of the game her shoulders ached from hunching over and her hand hurt from gripping the pencil. She double-checked everything she had written, erasing some entries and filling them in again, neater and clearer. Finally, she looked at the pages critically and nodded to herself.

It was the tidiest score sheet she had ever done. She could hardly wait to show it to Jim.

The next morning Maggie was at the firehouse bright and early. She had planned to look at the scorebook with Jim right then and there, but as she thrust it into his hands, she felt a little flutter in her stomach and went to pet Charky instead.

She held her breath as she heard him flip to the right pages. Would he think she had done a good job?

"What the heck . . . ," Jim muttered.

Maggie swallowed hard. Slowly she lifted her head.

"You gotta be kidding!" he said. He looked up from the score sheet, and his face lit up with a grin.

Maggie jumped to her feet and went to stand next to him. "I was worried it would make things too crowded," she said. "I been practicing writing as small as I can."

Not only had Maggie kept track of the plays the way he had taught her, she had added a couple touches of her own.

At the very bottom of each square, in the tiniest

letters she could manage, she had written the ball-and-strike count. "B" for a ball, "S" for a strike. A regular S for a swinging strike, a backward S for a strike looking: Ƨ.

"The pitch count!" Jim said. "For every single batter—that's just great! How'd you come up with that?"

Maggie felt floaty inside from his praise. "Well, I always love it when a guy gets a hit when he's got two strikes on him. I think that it's—um, it's really good batting, y'know? Good batting under pressure. So I wanted to be able to show that, but the only way to do it was to keep track of all the balls and strikes."

"I gotcha," Jim said. "Yeah, especially if there are runners on base and two out in a close game, that makes it really exciting, and it'd be great to know the count."

The second new thing was that some of the squares contained a tiny "x."

"What are the x's?" Jim asked. "No, wait, lemme see if I can figure it out." He narrowed his eyes and stared at the sheet.

Maggie waited, hopping up and down a little in her eagerness.

"Hmm . . . well, for a start, you've only got an x in the squares where the batter got a hit . . . the x's are all outside the diamond . . . only one x, never more than that. Wait, I think—"

He raised his eyebrows at her. "It's where the hit went, right?"

"Yep." A bigger hop—she couldn't help it. "Because sometimes a straight pull hitter goes to the opposite field—not often, but when it happens, it's interesting. And I figured . . . well, it didn't happen yesterday, but there might be other times when it would be good to know."

"Sure," Jim agreed. "I like a player who can hit to any field. They get that reputation, but it's good to have proof. That's what I like about keeping score. People talk a lot of malarkey about baseball, but when you score the games, you know what the truth is." He nodded. "You got a knack for it. When I was your age, I didn't even know how."

Maggie looked at him curiously. "Who taught you?" She had been meaning to ask him for a while.

Jim grinned. "My sister," he said. "See, when I was around your age, my dad tried to teach us, but I wasn't really interested. *She* was, even though she was younger'n me. Wasn't until high school that I finally decided I wanted to know how. My dad was gone by then, so I hadda ask her." A pause. "She taught me good. She still scores the games, too. When she can."

"What's her name?"

"Carol. She lives in Jersey, down the shore. Got two boys, little guys, younger than you—my nephews. I go see them once in a while."

"That's nice."

"Yeah. It's just her and me now. Mom passed a couple years ago."

"Oh." Maggie thought for a minute. Parents both dead, his sister living in another state—no wonder he spent so much time at the firehouse, sometimes even on his days off. But she was glad he did.

There was something else about keeping score—and Maggie loved this most of all. Like every other Dodger fan she knew, she felt almost like part of the team, like she herself was one of the Bums. It was as if cheering for them, supporting them, listening to the games, talking about them, somehow helped them play better.

Maggie knew that this didn't really make any sense. It wasn't like Jackie and Campy and Pee Wee *knew* that her radio was turned on, or played worse if it wasn't. But there were times when it felt as though the strength of her wishes, combined with those of thousands of other fans all over Brooklyn, pulled the player or the bat or the ball in the right direction—for a stolen base or a hit or a strikeout, exactly when it was needed most.

And for Maggie, keeping score of the game was way better than just listening. She was actually *doing* something. Which meant that she was helping even more than everyone else.

Three

THE NEW FAVORITE

*I*t was late July, and Friday would be Joey-Mick's twelfth birthday. Maggie knew exactly what she wanted to give him: a score sheet for one of his league games.

Just the way she'd planned it, Joey-Mick noticed her writing during one of the Dodger games and asked what she was doing. When she showed him, he was very impressed and said he wanted to learn. His penmanship was dreadful, though, and he couldn't write the numbers and letters small enough to fit in the squares. Then he pretended he wasn't really interested. But Maggie had seen him looking in her scorebook several times after Dodgers games, and she knew he'd love to have the score of one of his own games.

He had a game coming up on Wednesday. She could keep score, take some time on Thursday to make the score sheet look really nice, and give it to him on Friday.

But what if he had a terrible game? What if he

struck out twice and hit into a double play and made two errors in the field? His next game wouldn't be until Saturday, which meant she'd have to give him his present late—and besides, there was no guarantee he'd play well on Saturday, either.

Before Maggie got the idea of giving him a score sheet, she had been stuck for a while wondering what she could *buy* him. That summer, for the first time ever, she was getting spending money.

Dad gave her fifteen cents a week. She had to put a nickel in the church plate on Sunday, which left ten cents. A matinee movie ticket cost a quarter, but Mom almost always went to the movies too, so she paid for the tickets even after Maggie started getting an allowance.

That meant Maggie had enough for a candy bar every week. Or ten pieces of penny candy, her usual choice, because licorice sticks and bubblegum lasted longer than a Hershey bar. She gave up candy for three whole weeks, but there still wasn't much she could buy Joey-Mick for thirty cents. Especially when what he wanted was new sneakers and a genuine Dodgers cap and, most of all, to attend a Dodgers game at Ebbets Field.

That last wish wasn't something she could give him even if she had the money. Ebbets Field was only a couple of miles from their home, but neither Joey-Mick nor Maggie had ever been to a game there.

It was, in their opinion, their father's single major failing. He refused to let them go to a game at Ebbets Field. The question never even came up anymore;

he had made his refusal clear beyond all hope of discussion.

Why? Well, fire was one thing. Dad had seen plenty of fires and accidents and other disasters. But fire plus *a crowd:* That was his real nightmare.

A few years ago, there had been a fire at a circus in Connecticut. Dad was still at the firehouse back then, and some of the Brooklyn fire companies had gotten the call to help.

More than 160 people in the main tent had died. The fire itself caused some of the deaths, but it was the stampeding of the panicked crowd that killed many more. People running and screaming, tripping and falling in their hurry to try to escape the flames, and then getting trampled on by the rest of the crowd. Stepped on and kicked and crushed by dozens, even hundreds of other people. . . . Maggie couldn't imagine it, what it would be like to die that way.

Dad didn't have to imagine it. He had seen the bodies. Maggie knew it must have been awful beyond words, because Dad was such a talker, he loved telling stories—but he almost never talked about that day. Once when the subject came up, Maggie had seen that his eyes were blank and pained at the same time—like he was trying to pull a shade down over whatever was in his mind.

So Joey-Mick and Maggie weren't allowed to go to any events where a big crowd would be packed into a tight space. Which meant no major league games. Not even when Joey-Mick's friend Davey offered him a *free* ticket to a game last year courtesy of Davey's rich banker uncle—seats just beyond the Dodgers' dugout! Joey-Mick had said no without even asking. That was how ironclad the rule was.

Thank goodness for the radio. Some folks, like Mr. Marshall next door, could watch the games on television. Two years ago, Maggie's family along with half the neighborhood had crowded in to the Marshalls' living room to see a game on the brand-new RCA television set. Maggie had been terribly disappointed. Although the console was an enormous piece of furniture, the picture itself was only a small square, the players grainy and blurry in black and white. Nothing like the big screen at the movie theater. Maggie had gone home after only half an inning; she much preferred listening to the radio and imagining what the plays looked like.

And now they all went to see Joey-Mick's games twice a week. Maggie wished she had gotten the scoresheet idea sooner. She could have kept score last Saturday, when Joey-Mick had hit two singles and driven in three runs and been part of two double plays in the field. That would have been the perfect game to score—why hadn't she thought of it before?

Too bad. She would just have to score Wednesday's game and hope he did well. And if he didn't, she'd have to give him a dumb present like a Hershey bar. Which was what she had given him last year.

On Thursday morning Maggie took her notebook and walked down to the firehouse.

"Hey, Maggie-o! What are you doing here this time of day?" Jim greeted her. The Dodgers' game wasn't until later that afternoon.

"I wanted to show you something," she said. "I was hoping you might have an idea. . . ." She held out her notebook, open to the pages where she had scored Joey-Mick's game the evening before.

Jim took it and looked it over. "They won, eh? Good job. Looks like a pretty good game."

"Pitchers' duel," Maggie said, "one-nothing. Nobody scored until the fifth." One of Joey-Mick's teammates had hit a double, the opposing team had made not one but *two* errors on the play, and the run scored. Maggie could remember without looking at the score sheet, but it was all there in the tiny box:

"So what's the problem?" Jim asked.

Maggie explained about the birthday present.

"Yeah, your dad told me," Jim said. "He's gonna be twelve, right?" Then he grinned. "That's a great idea for a present. Man, I wish I had the score sheet for one of my games back when I was playing."

Jim had already told Maggie that he had been a pitcher on his high school team. Pitcher and third base, because he had a good arm. Not good enough for professional ball, though.

"See, there really wasn't too much going on in the game," Maggie said. "The pitchers kept getting everyone out. Including Joey-Mick."

"Well . . . did he do anything in the field?"

Maggie brightened. "Yeah. He made one really great play. In the third inning. He had to dive to catch a liner that was headed for the hole—stretched himself all the way out, landed flat on his stomach. But he held on to the ball!"

She grinned proudly, seeing the play in her head again. "Saved a run from scoring, too." Then she sighed. "But I don't know how to show what a good play it was. I mean, right now, it just says '4' in the box." 4, for an out made by the second baseman.

Jim nodded. "I see what you mean. But don't worry, we'll think of something. . . ."

Maggie scissored the two pages carefully out of her notebook. She taped them together along the cut edges so the pages would open like a card. Then she wrote *Happy Birthday, Joey-Mick, from Maggie* on one of the blank sides. She thought about drawing balloons on it, too, but decided he would think that was babyish.

On Friday they had ice cream for dessert, Joey-Mick's brick with a candle stuck in it. Then he opened his presents. Dad gave him the coveted genuine Dodgers' cap. Mom had made two pennant-shaped banners for him to hang on the wall above his bed. One was dark blue with white lettering—DODGERS. The other was red with black letters—WILDCATS, the name of Joey-Mick's own team. Mom was good at sewing and knitting and things like that, and the banners looked almost exactly like store-bought ones.

Maggie handed Joey-Mick the score sheet and

watched eagerly as he opened it. She saw his eyes move as he glanced down one page, then the next.

He looked up and grinned at her. "Thanks, Mags," he said.

That was all, but she had seen the pride in his grin. It was exactly what she'd been hoping for. It meant he had seen the little box with the play in the third inning, which, thanks to a brilliant idea from Jim, now looked like this:

```
┌──────────┐
│    4!     │
│ B2       │
└──────────┘
```

A few days later, Maggie stood on the front stoop watching as Joey-Mick slammed the ball against the bottom step. "That's the dumbest thing I ever heard!" he yelled.

The ball rebounded at a crazy angle, flew through the air, and hit the rear fender of the car parked nearby. Mr. Marshall's brand-new Buick. If he wasn't driving it, he was outside wiping it down with a cloth or inside staring at it from the front window. It was a nice car all right, long and gray with sleek fins that made Maggie think of a shark. But the way he fussed over it, you'd have thought it was a puppy or a baby or something.

Maggie glanced anxiously over at Mr. Marshall's house. She held her breath for a moment, but it seemed that he wasn't sitting at the window. Meanwhile, Joey-Mick ran over and checked the car's bumper. No mark.

He glared at her. "See what you made me do?" he said over his shoulder as he went to fetch the ball.

"I didn't make you do it," she protested. "You threw the ball your own self."

"Yeah, but it was your fault! You say stupid things like that, what am I supposed to do?"

"It's not stupid!"

"For gosh sake, Maggie!" Joey-Mick retrieved the ball from the gutter. As he walked back toward her, he took off his cap and wiped his brow with one angry swipe of his arm. "You think you know so much about baseball—well, this just proves you don't know hardly nothing!"

"It's not like there's no *rule* about it, Joey-Mick."

"Yes, there is! Just because something's not written down somewheres don't mean it's not a rule! You can't have a favorite player who's not on your favorite team! It don't make any sense!"

His face was red now from all the yelling he was doing. "Besides, it's *double* stupid to pick a player on your worst-enemy team! Any idiot would know that!"

Maggie sighed. She knew it was no use arguing with him, but she couldn't stop herself from trying. "Look, I got it all figured out. I always root for the Dodgers to win. Cross my heart and hope to die." She crossed her heart with a quick motion. "But I can root for *him* to do good at the same time. Even if they're playing each other, he could have a good game and the Dodgers could still win, see?"

"No, I don't see! I mean, *you're* the one who don't

see! If *he* does good, then the Giants do good too, don't you get it?" He began *thunk*ing the ball into his glove the way he always did, but much harder than usual, as if it could help him pound some sense into her. *THUNK—THUNK.*

Maggie shook her head and stuck out her chin. She could be just as stubborn as him when she wanted to be.

Joey-Mick stopped *thunk*ing the ball into his glove long enough to put his hand on her shoulder. "Look, Mags," he said, his voice gentle now. "You gotta keep Campy as your favorite player, okay? You were so-o-o smart to pick him, and look how good he's been doing! You can't switch now—it's bad luck for the team, and I know you wouldn't want that."

Maggie pulled away from his hand. She'd rather he kept yelling; she hated when he talked to her all kind and patient like that. Like she was a baby.

"Treecie's still got Campy as her favorite," she said, her own voice rising now. "You just mind your own business. I'm telling you, Willie Mays is my favorite player, and there's nothing you can do about it!"

She spun away from him and went into the house, slamming the door behind her.

Willie Mays. She had learned all about him while scoring Giants games with Jim. The way he played, for one thing. *Fast*—whether in center field or on the base paths. The radio announcers said that he ran so fast, he sometimes ran right out from under his cap. Maggie loved hearing that; it was as if there was so much joy in his playing that he couldn't contain it—and since he couldn't quite fly himself, his cap flew instead.

His hitting was good—not spectacular yet, but Jim said that would come with time. "Heck," he said, "the kid's only twenty years old. You just wait. He's gonna be one of the greats."

Maggie believed him, and she believed in Willie Mays. Already there were lots of stories about him. Like how he could hold *five* baseballs in one hand. "That's how come he can throw the ball so good," Jim said. "Them big hands—he can really get a grip on the ball, put any kind of spin on it he wants."

Like how his batting average had been an incredible .477 with his minor-league team in Minneapolis. And even though he'd only been with that team for a couple of months, the fans there were crazy about him. When the Giants called him to come to New York in May, their owner, Horace Stoneham, took out a huge ad in the Minneapolis newspaper, explaining why he was taking Willie away.

Like how in Minneapolis Willie once hit a ball so hard that it went right *through* the board fence in the outfield, and they didn't fix the hole—they left it there for the rest of the season and even painted a circle around it.

Like how he hadn't been sure about leaving Minneapolis and going to the Giants because he didn't think he could hit big-league pitching, and in the beginning it looked as if he might be right. He got only one hit in his first twenty-six tries—it was a home run, but still, only one hit in all those at-bats—and he was so discouraged that he thought maybe he should go back to the minors. But Giants manager Leo Durocher kept him in New York, and Willie finally started hitting and didn't stop. Maggie had felt an almost terrified relief when Jim told her that story. If Willie had gone back to the minors in May, she would probably never even have heard of him; she hadn't started listening to the Giants games until July.

Now he was her favorite player. He gave her the same kind of shivery feeling she got when she heard Jackie Robinson's name during the broadcast of a game. Something was going to happen—maybe something good, but even if it wasn't good, it would be something exciting. That was what it was like with Jackie and Willie.

She had known that picking Willie as her favorite would cause trouble with Joey-Mick and sure enough, she was right. Now she was going to have to tell about arguing with him when she went to confession on Saturday.

She hoped it would be Father John in the confessional. Maybe he would go easy on her; of all the parish priests, he was the biggest baseball fan.

In August, the Giants had won an amazing, unbelievable *sixteen games in a row*. The Dodgers' gargantuan lead of 13 games over the Giants in the standings was shriveling away, bit by agonizing bit.

It wasn't that the Dodgers were playing all that badly. During the Giants' winning streak, the Dodgers won nine games and lost eight. Not wonderful, but not a disaster either—still above .500.

But the Giants! It was like they had forgotten how to lose!

And Willie—Willie was part of making it happen. Maggie's score sheets for the Giants' games were littered with exclamation points for his terrific plays in the outfield. On the bases, he ran so hard that he turned singles into doubles—twenty-two of them, fourth best on the team, even though he was only a rookie—and doubles into triples, that rarest and most exciting of hits. Five of them that year, when most players were lucky to hit five in a lifetime. Jim said that if Willie didn't win Rookie of the Year, he'd eat his hat.

"My *work* hat," he said, and pointed to his fireman's helmet hanging on the wall. Maggie had laughed at the time, but she wasn't laughing now. Joey-Mick's words were haunting her.

If he does good, the Giants do good, too, don't you get it?

You can't switch now, it's bad luck for the team. . . .

In desperation, she tried a new tactic: not listening to Giants games. She knew how to score almost everything; she hardly ever had to ask Jim for help anymore, and if she didn't know something, she could always ask him later.

Only Dodger games from now on. Maybe that would help get them out of their slump.

She told Jim that she wouldn't be coming to the firehouse for the Giants' broadcasts, at least for a while. He nodded in understanding.

"But don't be a stranger around here, Maggie-o," he said.

"I won't," she promised. "I'll stop by so you can tell me how Willie's doing."

He cocked his head at her. "We can do better than that," he said. He went into the firehouse and came back with a newspaper.

"There's a story about the Giants every day," he said, holding the paper out toward her. "Dodgers, too. Handy if you can't hear the game, but even if I do, I like to read what the paper says anyways."

"You don't have to give me yours," Maggie said. Dad stopped at a newsstand every evening on his way back from work and brought the paper home.

"Fine, but just lemme show ya," Jim said.

They sat down and looked at the paper together. The biggest stories on the front page were about President Truman at some meeting in San Francisco, and the war in Korea. Jim showed her where the table of contents was, in tiny print near the bottom. "This way you can go right to the sports pages," he said.

To Maggie's delight, there were not only stories about the games played by the three New York teams but also the box scores for every major league game, and statistics for batting and pitching. Of course she had known there was baseball news in the paper. But the newspaper had always seemed like something for grownups; she had never thought of reading it herself.

Overnight Maggie became a newspaper addict. Not the whole paper, of course. Just the sports section. And just the baseball part of the sports section. Dad always gave the paper to Mom when he got home, and Mom put it aside until after dinner, when she could sit for a while and read it in peace. She was cross when she caught Maggie taking the sports pages.

"Leave that paper be," Mom said.

"But it's only the sports," Maggie said.

"I don't like the paper messed with. You leave it be until I'm done."

It wasn't fair. Why should Mom care so long as Maggie took just the sports pages? But she had to wait until Mom was finished. After that, Maggie could do as she pleased with the paper.

She started clipping articles about the Dodgers and kept them in her scoring notebook. Listening to the games on the radio, scoring the games, reading the articles, clipping them—she was doing everything she could to help stop the Dodgers' lead from dwindling away.

Four

PLAYOFF

*N*one of those things mattered. At the end of the regular season, the Dodgers and the Giants were tied for the lead in the National League. That thirteen-game lead was gone, as if it had never existed. The two teams would play an extra three-game series to determine the league champion.

Maggie bought a new notebook especially for the playoff games. She thought maybe a nice clean notebook—getting away from the losses recorded in the old one—would bring the Dodgers good luck.

She decided to try something else too, to help the team.

The night before the playoffs, Maggie turned off her bedside lamp, crossed herself, laced her fingers together, and closed her eyes.

When she was little, bedtime prayers had been part of getting tucked in. Either Mom or Dad would sit on the edge of the bed as Maggie squeezed her eyes shut and folded her hands and said, "Dear God, please bless

Mommy and Daddy and Joey-Mick and me and all our friends and relations and the most abandoned souls in Purgatory. Amen." The sheet got pulled up and her forehead got kissed and the light got turned out, the same routine every night. Maggie was too old now for tucking-in, but she still said her prayers.

She lay there and took a breath before starting. Then she whispered the words into the darkness. "Please God bless Mom and Dad and Joey-Mick and me and all our friends and relations and the most abandoned souls in Purgatory and—and the Dodgers. Amen."

Maggie squeezed her hands together a little harder. Would God be cross with her for praying about baseball? After all, it was just a game. . . . He had an awful lot of more important things to take care of. Every week in church, Father John or one of the other priests asked for intercessions, and then everyone prayed for other people. Usually the intercessions were for people who were sick or hurt. Or had lost their jobs, or gone off to Korea to fight in the war. A few times, Maggie's dad had asked for prayers for a fireman who had been injured at work.

And once, Mom had done the asking. When Dad got hurt.

Maggie opened her eyes. In the darkness there were darker shapes—the dresser, the chair with her robe on it.

She had never heard anyone ask for prayers for a sports team.

But just suppose that God didn't mind hearing

prayers for sports teams. Wouldn't Giants fans be praying to Him, too? Did God like one team more than another?

If that were true, then God had to be a Yankee fan.

For a moment, Maggie felt almost angry. But the anger was mixed up with confusion and, well, fear. You weren't supposed to get mad at God.

"Sorry," she whispered.

She felt a tiny bit better, but not any less confused.

If God *did* care about baseball, then it sure looked like He cared more about the Yankees than the Dodgers. And what about teams like the Pirates, who year after year lost more games than they won—a *lot* more. Didn't God care about the Pirates or their fans at all?

The morning of the first playoff game, Joey-Mick spent a good few minutes trying to figure out which shirts he had been wearing during the Dodgers' wins and losses; he wanted to throw the losingest one away. Mom rescued the green striped shirt as Joey-Mick was going out the door with it, headed for the garbage can back behind the house.

"I never heard such nonsense," she scolded. "That shirt cost good money—do you think your father works so hard just to have you make a fuss over a silly game!" She flapped the shirt angrily.

"I'm not wearing it ever again," Joey-Mick muttered.

Maggie left her mother and brother glowering at each other in the front hall and ran up the stairs to his bedroom. She opened one of Joey-Mick's drawers in the bureau, found what she was looking for right on top, and took it downstairs.

"Here, Joey-Mick," she said, holding out a blue-and-white plaid. "You should wear this one." He had been wearing it the day before when the Dodgers beat the Phillies, 9–8, on an impossible, incredible, game-winning home run by none other than Jackie Robinson. It had taken the Bums fourteen innings to win—Maggie's score sheet covered four pages of the notebook instead of the usual two—and the victory had kept them in the race. If they had lost, the Giants would have won the title outright, without the need for the three-game playoff.

She handed Joey-Mick the shirt. "It's the right color too," she added. Dodger blue.

He took it and stomped off. Maggie sighed. They hadn't talked about Willie Mays since their argument, but she knew that Joey-Mick was still mad at her. The whole thing probably would have blown over if it hadn't been for the way the pennant race was going. Every time Red Barber announced another Giants win during the broadcast of a Dodgers game, Joey-Mick would glare at her and shake his head.

Usually Maggie ignored him. It was just a coincidence that she had picked Willie as her favorite player right as the Giants started winning like crazy. Her choice didn't make one bit of difference to the way they were playing—it wasn't like Willie *knew* she had picked him. Or that he'd play any better if he did know.

But sometimes she caught herself feeling a little guilty. Could picking Willie as her favorite player really have put a jinx on the Dodgers?

It was too late now anyway. Willie was her favorite, and there wasn't anything she could do to change the way she felt. If she had said that she was going back to Roy Campanella, it would have been a lie; inside, Willie would still be her favorite, and then she'd have the lie as well as the jinx on her conscience.

There was one thing she could do, though. During the playoffs, she planned to cheer for Brooklyn as hard as she possibly could. Willie had already had a great season. Three more games weren't going to change that.

She would cheer for the Dodgers, not for Willie. Every minute of every game.

Maggie ran home from school as fast as she could in an effort to catch at least the last inning. Treecie ran with her as far as the corner, then had to turn down the street to go home and look after her sisters. *"Go, Dodgers!"* Treecie shouted as Maggie raced away. Maggie waved over her shoulder.

At home she rushed into the living room. Mom was sitting on the sofa, knitting, and Joey-Mick was there, too. Not only that, but the game had just ended: The Dodgers had lost, 3–1. At Ebbets Field—their own home ground.

Joey-Mick yelled at Maggie that it had been a dumb idea for him to wear the blue plaid shirt. Maggie yelled back that she hadn't made him wear it;

he could have worn something else. Joey-Mick ripped off the shirt so fast that two of the buttons popped. Then he threw it at Maggie. It didn't hurt, but she started to cry anyway, which made Mom put down her knitting.

Maggie flung herself at Mom and held on, sobbing.

"For shame, Joseph Michael, making her cry so," Mom said as she patted Maggie's back with one hand and moved her knitting out of the way with the other.

"I didn't do nothin'! She's just a big baby."

"It's not him," Maggie choked out. She took a second out from crying to scowl at her brother. Then she turned back to Mom, and the tears started up again. "They lost—s-so they'll have to play the next two games at—at the stupid Polo Grounds, with all the—the stupid Giants' fans there—it's not f-fair—"

"Ah, for the love of Kerry," Mom said, "it's only a game, what are you in such a stew about?"

Maggie only cried harder. She was crying because the Dodgers had lost; because they had blown such a huge lead in the standings; because not listening to the Giants' games and getting a new notebook and picking the right shirt hadn't helped. But most of all she was crying because her mother just didn't understand.

"It's not fair," she said again, her words muffled in Mom's blouse.

After a few moments, Maggie's sobs slowed a little.

"Now, then," Mom said crisply, "enough of that. It's that fine young Mr. Labine pitching tomorrow. I like the way he's been throwing. So stop your belly-aching and leave go of me. I've work to do."

Maggie had indeed stopped crying. She was staring up at Mom's face with her mouth and eyes wide open. Mom gave her shoulder a quick pat-slap and went back to her knitting.

Maggie and Joey-Mick looked at each other in silent amazement.

Mom knew *a lot* about the Dodgers. Clem Labine was a rookie; he had pitched in only a dozen or so games that year. You'd have had to be paying pretty good attention to know about him.

Something fell into place in Maggie's head as neatly as the last piece of a jigsaw puzzle. Dad was a Yankee fan. But as far back as Maggie could remember, when she and Joey-Mick were barely more than babies, it had been the *Dodgers'* games that sounded from the radio. And with Dad away at work all day, that could mean only one thing.

Mom was a Dodger fan.

She doesn't make a lot of noise about it, the way the rest of us do, Maggie thought. *That's just her way. . . . I wonder who her favorite player is.*

On the day of the second playoff game, Maggie and Joey-Mick arrived home at the same time and found the radio on full blast, Mom hanging wet laundry out back as she listened to the broadcast through the open window. The yard behind the house was just a patch of cement with a revolving clothesline planted in the middle, which Dad always called their tree because there was no other tree in the yard. The clothesline did have a center pole for a trunk and supports for branches, with the laundry like big leaves flapping in the breeze. "Hey, Maggie-o, pick a shirt off the tree for me," he would say.

There wasn't even time for Maggie to get her scorebook; the game was almost over. Maggie already knew that the Dodgers were winning. As usual, she had been able to hear the broadcast from radios all along the street during her run home from school.

The final out! Joey-Mick jumped to his feet and they danced around the room together, shouting and laughing, and then out the door into the yard, where he grabbed hold of a pair of Dad's dungarees pinned to the line and flung them so that the whole revolving clothesline started spinning madly, and he and Maggie ran in circles around it.

"Joseph Michael!" Mom yelled. Then she had to duck out of the way as the wet dungarees sailed toward her head, and finally she was laughing too. When they had all calmed down a little and were picking up the socks that had whirled off the line, Mom shook a finger at them and said, "Mr. Labine. Did I not tell you?"

Clem Labine's beautiful pitching and a barrage of hits by his teammates had added up to a 10–0 victory over the Giants, Brooklyn piling up run after run as if they would never stop scoring. Game 2 to the Dodgers! The winner of Game 3 would be league champion and go on to play in the World Series!

*   *   *

The morning of the third game, Maggie and Joey-Mick grinned at each other as they left for school. They had just emerged in triumph after a fierce discussion with Mom about staying home from school after lunch so they could listen to the game. "Oh, suit yourselves, then!" Mom snapped in the end, but Maggie had the feeling she wasn't nearly as cross as she sounded.

The radio was turned up loud enough so Mom could hear it in the kitchen. Maggie sat in the green armchair as usual, busy with score sheet and pencil. Joey-Mick lounged on the rug and plunked the ball into his glove, *thunk—thunk—thunk*. Maggie was so used to the sound that she hardly heard it. But whenever Joey-Mick stopped during an exciting play so he could concentrate on listening, she always noticed the gap in that steady beat.

As the bottom of the ninth inning approached, Maggie and Joey-Mick were both fidgeting to contain their joy. The Dodgers had scored three runs in the eighth inning to take the lead, 4–1. Just three more outs and the pennant would be theirs.

The Giants started the inning with two straight hits, followed by an out and a double that drove in a run. But just one; the Dodgers were still ahead, 4–2. Only two outs to go.

With two men on base, Bobby Thomson would be the next batter. Pitcher Ralph Branca came in to relieve starter Don Newcombe.

"Branca?" Joey-Mick exclaimed.

"It'll be okay," Maggie said immediately. She knew what Joey-Mick was thinking: In Game 1 of the playoffs, Thomson had faced Branca and hit a two-run homer. "It'll never happen twice in a row."

Joey-Mick nodded.

But if Thomson did manage to get on base, the next batter would be . . . Willie Mays. When Red Barber announced that Willie was on deck, Joey-Mick glared at Maggie so fiercely that she could feel the heat of it on the back of her neck when she bent her head down to her score sheet again.

First pitch to Thomson, a strike. Maggie recorded it dutifully. She wrote a backward S very, very slowly: *If I write it slow enough and the next pitch comes before I finish, it'll be another strike.* The whole game had been filled with thoughts like that: *If I wait one more batter to get a drink of water, the Dodgers will get him out. . . . If I don't change positions until the end of the inning, the Dodgers will score a run.*

She had to cheat and add a tiny extra curl to the tail of the S so she wouldn't lift the pencil until the next pitch. Then she looked up at the radio.

"Branca pumps . . . delivers . . . a curve ball. A deep fly to left field—it is . . . a home run! And the New York Giants win the National League pennant, and the crowd goes wild. . . ."

Red Barber said nothing more for what felt like ages. All Maggie could hear was the crowd's roar, so loud and incessant that it sounded almost like static, as if the radio was stuck between stations, the noise a perfect match for the buzzing numbness inside her head.

The Polo Grounds had the shortest left-field fence

in all of baseball. If the game had been at Ebbets Field—if it had been *anywhere* else—that hit would never have been a home run. Andy Pafko would have caught it easy as pie.

But it *was* the Polo Grounds. Game over: Giants 5, Dodgers 4.

Later, Maggie would learn that the Giants' announcer Russ Hodges had screamed over and over, "THE GIANTS WIN THE PENNANT! THE GIANTS WIN THE PENNANT!"—four times altogether, at the top of his lungs. She would also hear that Jackie Robinson had refused to leave the field until Thomson touched all four bases; if he hadn't, the fifth run wouldn't have counted. Jackie was a fighter, that was for sure. Right to the end, and even after the end.

But for now, she sat frozen, pencil in hand, unable to score the final play of the game. *If I don't write it down, maybe it didn't happen.* The shock had paralyzed Joey-Mick too; neither of them could move enough to turn off the radio.

A ridiculous thought came to Maggie through the numbness. Willie Mays hadn't been involved at all, hadn't come to bat during that awful, horrible, terrible, dreadful inning. Suppose Willie had ended up being the hero instead of Bobby Thomson—what would she have done then?

On second thought, she probably wouldn't have had time to worry about it. Joey-Mick would have killed her first.

* * *

Dazed, Maggie closed her notebook without scoring Thomson's home run. Joey-Mick jumped to his feet and went upstairs without a word. As he left the room, his face was white and stony, as if it was about to break into a million pieces. Although she couldn't hear him, Maggie was sure he was crying. Probably lying on his bed with the pillow over his head.

She couldn't remember the last time he had cried about anything.

Maggie sat there for a while thinking about her prayers. They hadn't worked for the first game, so she had almost decided not to pray for the Dodgers the night before the second game. But at the last minute she had changed her mind. She had done it once, and if she didn't do it again, maybe God would think she hadn't meant it the first time.

The Dodgers had won the second game! So Maggie had prayed again before the third game.

And look what happened.

It hadn't worked.

It *really* hadn't worked. Ahead until the last swing of the bat and then losing—that was maybe the hardest way of all to lose.

What had gone wrong? Were there more Giants fans who had said prayers than Dodgers fans?

Then Mom called from the kitchen, "Turn off that radio, Margaret Olivia. It's giving me a headache."

Mom didn't use Maggie's full name very often. Only when she was angry. *She's not mad at me,* Maggie thought. *It's the game. She's upset about it, too.*

Maggie found that her legs were shaky when she stood and crossed the room. So was her hand as she reached to turn off the Philco. It was strange that she didn't feel like crying herself. In her brain she knew that the Dodgers had lost, but somehow the news hadn't reached her heart yet. Inside she was just . . . empty.

Suddenly, she had to get out of the house. She knew exactly what to do: She had to go to the firehouse and hug Charky. And then maybe take him for a walk.

"I'll be back soon," she mumbled to her mother.

Mom nodded, then said, "There's an end from the bologna." Maggie looked at her gratefully and took the scrap of meat from the Frigidaire.

The street was ominously quiet; all the radios had been turned off. Maggie didn't stop at any of the shops to say hello. *If anyone looks at me, I probably* will *start crying.*

Charky met her half a block from the firehouse. As always he was tongue-and-tail delighted to see her. Maggie knelt on the sidewalk to give him the bologna. He snapped down the treat while she hugged him fiercely. Then he pranced by her side as she walked on. "You'd be even happier if the Dodgers had won, wouldn't you, boy?" she murmured. "Wait till next year, Charks."

As Maggie neared the firehouse, she could see George and Vince and Terry sitting in front of the bay doors. Jim wasn't there. Maggie was ashamed of the relief she felt, but she didn't think she could face a

Giants fan right now. Not even one who was as good a friend as Jim.

"Hey, Maggie-o," George said, but without his usual cheer. The other two greeted her as well, both solemn.

"Hi," she said. And couldn't think of one more word to say.

She went inside the bay doors to fetch Charky's leash.

"Helluva thing," she heard George say. "Just when you thought the day couldn't get any worse."

"Hey," Terry said. "Don't talk like that. It don't mean nothin' yet. We don't even know—heck, he might not get anywhere near the fighting."

What were they talking about? Maggie came out with the leash in her hand. Charky bounded around her. "Down, Charks," she said absently. "George?"

George cleared his throat and looked down at the ground.

"Might as well tell her," Terry said. "She's gonna find out soon enough. Besides, he'd probably want her to know."

He? Who—Jim? Find out what?

George raised his head. "Yeah, Maggie-o, it's Jim. He left right after the game." He paused. Maggie waited in silence, but she was starting to feel itchy.

"He's somethin', our Jim," George went on at last. "The game ends, right? And he asks if he can leave his shift a little early, so he can go celebrate with—with his *Giants* friends." George said the word "Giants" like it tasted bad. "Then he takes this envelope out of his pocket and sorta waves it at us. 'Gotta get in some good times pretty quick,' he says."

George shook his head. "Helluva thing," he said again.

Terry spoke up. "It was his call-up notice."

"His what?" Maggie asked.

"Army," George said. "Jim's been drafted. He's going to Korea. To the war."

Five

DEAR JIM

1952–53

"You're gonna write to him, aren't you?" Treecie asked.

They were in Mr. Aldo's shop on an errand for Maggie's mom.

Maggie picked out a can of baked beans. "Of course," she said. "As soon as he leaves. Next week sometime."

Before Christmas, Jim had been to basic training camp for several weeks. He was home now for a quick visit; he would be shipping out to Korea very soon.

January—a bad time of year now made even worse, Maggie thought. Whenever baseball season ended, the six months without games felt like a long straight road stretching to a pinpoint on the horizon and beyond it—a road that would never end. November and December weren't too bad; there were all the holidays plus Maggie's and Treecie's birthdays. But New Year's Day was followed by three and a half torturous months: short gray days, cold dull weather, and no baseball. How would she ever get through it?

"Keep busy" was what Mom would say.

Maggie snapped her fingers. "You know what I could do? I could write to him and mail it even before he leaves, and that way it'll get there right when he does and it'll be a big surprise!"

"But where will you send it?"

Maggie hadn't thought of that. How did soldiers get their mail? "I'll ask my dad," she said.

Sure enough, Dad knew what to do: He called Jim's sister in New Jersey to get the address. Dad kept in touch with most of "his boys"—the guys he had hired to be new firemen—but not usually with their families; Maggie was surprised that he knew Jim's sister.

When she asked Dad about it, he said, "She's the only folks he's got left." Maggie knew that, and she thought she understood what Dad meant by saying it: that he was keeping an extra-close eye on Jim. Probably even more so because Jim worked at Dad's old firehouse.

The address was a ship that would leave from Seattle in Washington State. She had never sent a letter to a ship before. And Seattle seemed so far away; it was hard to imagine that Jim would be crossing the whole country and then crossing a whole ocean as well.

January 6, 1952

Dear Jim,

You want to know something funny? I'm writing this letter at the firehouse and you're sitting right next to me! You're

*reading the paper and I think you think
I'm doing my homework. . . .*

Maggie didn't have much to write about since he hadn't even left yet, so she thanked him again for the present he had given her for her birthday: a photograph of Willie Mays. At the bottom was a caption: "Willie Mays, the 'Say-Hey' Kid," and underneath that, "N.L. Rookie of the Year—1951." Jim had explained that when Willie couldn't remember someone's name, he always called out, "Say hey," and that was how he got his nickname.

The photo was taped to the wall above her bed now, and Willie smiled at her every night before she turned out the light.

The firehouse guys had a little goodbye party for Jim. A tray of cold cuts and rolls, and bottles of soda, and folks from the neighborhood stopping in at the end of the day. Maggie and Treecie handed out sodas and napkins; Maggie fed Charky bits from the tray.

As people left, they shook Jim's hand.

"Give those Commies what-for, Jim."

"You show them reds who's boss."

"They're nothin' but yella cowards, Jim. Make 'em run."

Maggie stayed until the end with Dad and helped clean up. Finally, Jim said it was time for him to go. He had to be up early the next day to catch a train.

He shook hands with George and Vince and Terry.

"They won't know what hit 'em," George declared.

"Nobody makes a better soldier than a smoke-eater, and that's a fact. You're gonna do us proud, Jim."

Dad shook Jim's hand and gave him a bear hug and a clap on the back.

Maggie wondered what she should do—shake his hand? Or hug him? Sometimes George gave her a hug, but that was different; she had known him since she was a baby. She didn't have to decide right away, because the next thing Jim did was drop to one knee.

"Hey Charks! C'mere, Charky-boy."

Somehow Charky knew it was a solemn moment, for he walked over instead of bounding, the way he usually did. He nosed Jim's hand, then licked it.

Jim rubbed the dog's neck with both hands. "Charky," he said, "see Maggie there?"

Charky knew her name. He looked at her and pranced in place a little but stayed where he was.

"You gotta keep her company now. When she's scoring a game, or goes for a walk. I'm countin' on you. Okay? Okay, boy?"

The dog barked twice in response. Everyone laughed, and Maggie knelt down to pet Charky, too. "Good boy," she said.

Jim reached over and ruffled her hair. "You take care, Maggie-o."

"You too, Jim."

"Keep them scorebooks up to date."

"I will," she promised.

Then Jim stood and saluted them all. He turned the salute into a little wave as he went out the door.

Charky barked again and ran to the door. Maggie followed him. Together they stood on the pavement and watched Jim walk down the street.

Maggie leaned her leg into the dog's warm fur. "He'll be back soon, Charks," she murmured. "And you know what? We'll have an even bigger party for him then."

With balloons. And me and Treece can make a big banner that says "Welcome home!" And maybe Mom will help me bake a cake. . . .

Jim wasn't even out of sight yet, and already she couldn't wait for him to come home.

One morning a couple of weeks after Maggie sent her letter, Treecie was waiting for her on their usual corner, where they met to walk to school together. Maggie started to run, waving an envelope in the air.

"Treece! He wrote back!"

> *January 14, 1952*
>
> *Dear Maggie-o,*
>
> *I'm writing this on the boat. I am VERY seasick. I can't hardly hold the pen, but I wanted to let you know that I got your letter and thanks for writing. It was a nice surprise to get a letter so soon after leaving home, I'm the only guy in our berth who got one already.*
>
> *Will write again when I'm feeling better. Sorry.*
>
> *Your friend Jim*

Treecie laughed. "Kinda short," she said.

"Yeah, but at least he wrote," Maggie said. She put the letter back in the envelope as they walked on.

"We should bake cookies and send them to him," Treecie said. "My mom told me about it once, it's called a CARE package. I forget what the letters stand for, but when you send food to army guys, that's a CARE package." During World War II, Treecie's mom had helped look after injured soldiers.

"That's a good name for it."

> *January 24, 1952*
>
> *Dear Jim,*
>
> *I was so sorry to hear that you were sick on the boat! I really really hope you're feeling better now.*
>
> *I didn't even know where Korea was but I looked it up in the atlas at school. Wow, it's really far away, almost exactly on the opposite side of the world from Brooklyn.*
>
> *Treecie and me made cookies for you, I hope they're not all crumbs by the time you get them. . . .*

Maggie wrote to Jim every week, sometimes even twice a week.

> *The new guy started this week. His name is Charlie. He's nice and everything, but I asked Dad and he said that you'll get your old job back when you come home and*

they'll find another house for Charlie. George says to tell you, Charlie's great because he's a Dodgers fan!

BIG NEWS, REALLY REALLY BIG! Maybe you heard it already but I wanted to write to you RIGHT AWAY in case you haven't, anyway here it is: WILLIE MAYS IS GOING INTO THE ARMY!!!!!
    CAN YOU BELIEVE IT!??!!!!!!
    He's supposed to leave in May! Maybe he'll be in your battalion! Wouldn't that be AMAZING!??!!

Opening Day! I thought it would NEVER get here! Dodgers opened two days ago and beat the Braves 3–2. Then—and I know this is the part you really want to hear—yesterday the Giants won their opening game against Philly 5–3. I kept score of the last two innings for you and I'll copy it and put it in with this letter. . . .

Jim wrote back every time. First about the ship, an enormous personnel carrier that had taken him and several hundred other soldiers to Japan.

The boat was something else. Wish I knew how big it was or how many people were on it all together, but maybe it's better I don't know. All that steel and everything, I felt like

*it oughtta sink right to the bottom. And I
was so sick, well anyway, I'm glad that trip
is over.*

And about the guys who shared the barracks with
him.

*I have five bunkmates and they're from all
over the place. So we got one Giants fan
(that's me of course), one Cubs fan, one
Indians fan, one Braves fan, one Red Sox
fan, and one Cardinals fan. It sure is different from being with Brooklyn fans all the
time.*

*Next time I write to you, it'll be from
Korea. We're supposed to ship out tomorrow.*

On a Saturday in late April, Maggie was sitting on the
stoop waiting for the mailman, Mr. Armstrong.
During the week the mail came while she was at
school. The first thing she always did when she walked
into the house was look on the hall table to see if there
was a letter from Jim.

But on Saturdays Mr. Armstrong arrived midmorn-
ing, and Maggie waited for him whenever she could.

"Letter from Korea!" he called out as soon as he
rounded the corner.

Maggie jumped up and ran to meet him. She knew
she still had to wait—the mail was all arranged in bun-
dles, it wouldn't be polite to ask him to find her letter

out of order—but walking alongside him was better than sitting.

"I always put it on top of your stack, when it's from overseas," Mr. Armstrong told her. He deposited a handful of mail through the slot of the house next door and burrowed into his bag again, right there on Mr. Marshall's stoop. "Here you go!"

Maggie grinned. "Thanks, Mr. Armstrong!" Nice of him to not make her wait even one more step. She took the pile of mail with one hand and waved goodbye with the other.

Back in her room, she held the envelope up to the light from the window before she opened it. Then she shook it a little. Yes, there was something inside, not just a letter.

A photograph!

A black-and-white photo. Jim, with his arm around the shoulders of a boy. A Chinese boy who looked about Maggie's age.

Not Chinese, silly. Korean.

> *We're all set up in camp now, outside a village. I've been assigned to an ambulance company. Tell Teeny Joe they said my fireman training would come in handy here.*
>
> *As soon as we got here we got ourselves a tent boy. His name is Jae-hyung, he's just a little bit older than you I think. He comes in the morning and collects our laundry and takes it home for his mom to do. He shines our boots too, cleans up around our tent,*

*stuff like that. Anyway the reason I'm telling
you about him is because we're teaching
him to play baseball. Mostly we just play
catch but sometimes there's enough of us for
a game.*

*Jay's learning English too, he catches on
real quick. I call him "Jay-Hey," because it
reminds me of Willie, the Say-Hey kid. I'm
sending you a picture of me and Jay-Hey in
front of our tent. . . .*

Maggie went down to the kitchen and came back
with a roll of tape. She put the photograph on her bedroom wall. Then she sat down to write to Jim.

Dear Jim,

*THANKS FOR THE PICTURE! I put it
up on my wall near the picture of Willie, so
now I have "Say-Hey" and "Jay-Hey" right
next to each other, ha ha!*

Maggie shared all of Jim's letters with Treecie. The
next time Treecie came over, Maggie showed her the
photo he had sent.

"Pretty good shot," Treecie said. "Good lighting on
their faces." She held it up and narrowed her eyes a little. "But they're too centered. I'd have shifted things so
they were more to the side. See, if the subject is off-
center, your eye gets drawn to it, so you have to look at
the whole thing, not just the middle."

Maggie hadn't even noticed whether Jim and Jay-Hey were in the middle or not. *Treecie sees the photo first. I see what's in the photo first.*

Jim and Jay were standing in front of a tent. The tent had a wooden door and a canvas roof. Jim was wearing his army uniform and a cap. Jay had on a white T-shirt and trousers the same shade as Jim's and a cap like Jim's too. A piece of heavy cord was tied tight around Jay's middle, scrunching up the waistband of the pants to make them fit.

Jim was smiling broadly. Jay was smiling too, but not as much; Maggie thought maybe he felt a little shy about having his picture taken.

She tilted her head at Treecie. "Do you think Jim's teaching him to keep score too? Or just how to play?"

Treecie rolled her eyes. "Are you crazy? *I* can't even keep score, and I've been a baseball fan for ages!"

They giggled. Maggie had tried to teach Treecie to keep score last season. After only a few minutes, Treecie had stopped the lesson and declared, "Sheesh. I like baseball, but not THIS much."

Maggie couldn't understand it. Keeping score was so much fun—how could anyone *not* want to do it?

"I wish it could be a job," she said now.

"You wish what could be a job?"

"Keeping score of Dodger games."

Treecie tapped her chin with one finger. "Maybe it is."

"Maybe it is what?"

"Well, you know the stuff in the newspaper, the

box scores and stuff you're always looking at? Somebody must keep track of all that." Treecie's eyes lit up. "Wow, if it *is* a job, it would be *perfect* for you!"

Maggie furrowed her brow. Treecie's words had brought to mind a certain kind of play. A batter would hit the ball, but it wouldn't go very far—it would stay in the infield. The batter would get to first base safely. Sometimes it was because the ball was hit in such a way that the fielder couldn't possibly reach it in time. That was scored as a hit. Other times, when the fielder messed up, it was an error. Maggie couldn't write the play down until the radio announcer said something like, "That'll be an error on the shortstop, according to the official scorer."

The official scorer. She had heard those words many times but had never really thought about them. Maybe Treecie was right—maybe scoring games *was* a job, and if it was, maybe it was something she could do when she grew up. It was the first time Maggie had given any serious thought to one of Treecie's career ideas.

"You know what would help him?" Treecie said. "Jay, I mean."

"Help him what?"

"Help him learn about baseball quicker. Baseball cards. You should send him some, I bet he'd like that."

Treecie was a genius, and Maggie told her so. In her next letter to Jim, Maggie sent two packs of baseball cards for Jay-Hey.

Jim's reply took longer than usual to arrive. For three Saturdays in a row, Mr. Armstrong called out

"Sorry, Maggie-o" as soon as he saw her. Then, on the last day of school, an envelope from Korea was waiting on the hall table.

> *Dear Maggie-o,*
>
> *Sorry I haven't written in a while, but I'll tell you why a little later in this letter. WOW, does Jay love those cards you sent. He looks at them a hundred times a day and asks me about a million questions about the stats! They're already getting pretty worn out and me too, I'm worn out from answering all his questions, ha ha.*
>
> *Anyway, me and Jay-Hey were working on something and it's finally ready, so that's why it's taken so long to send this letter. Turn over to see what it is. It took him a while to learn because our alphabet is different from theirs, but he wrote the whole thing himself.*
>
> *Happy 4th of July even though this might not get there in time.*
>
> *Your friend Jim*

Maggie turned the letter over. In the middle of the page was a note that had clearly been erased and rewritten several times.

> *To Maggie-o,*
> *Thanks for cards. I like!*
> *Jay*

"You could be pen pals!" Treecie said when she saw the note from Jay. "A pen pal from Korea, that would be SO neat."

Treecie had a pen pal who lived in Ohio, a girl named Martha whom she had met on Long Island two summers ago. Maggie wished she could have a girl for a pen pal. If she and Jay ended up writing to each other, maybe she could ask if he had a sister or a friend who was a girl. Then she would have *two* pen pals from Korea. *Maybe someday we could even visit each other—wouldn't that be amazing.*

Over the next few weeks, a flurry of small parcels left Brooklyn. Maggie continued to write to Jim, and in almost every letter she included something for Jay. Treecie came up with the idea of sending him a comic book. Maggie thought of a postcard showing the Statue of Liberty. She didn't wait for replies; whenever she or Treecie got an idea for something else to send him, Maggie wrote and sent it right away.

Treecie also took a photograph—a real one—of Maggie with the firehouse guys. Treece grumbled about the uselessness of her camera, something about the contrast in the photo not being quite right, but Maggie thought the picture was just fine and mailed it to Jim in her next letter.

Then Treecie went to Long Island for the summer. Maggie always missed her, but this year it seemed even worse than usual. After Treecie left, Maggie couldn't seem to think of anything else to send to Jay. The gift had to be inexpensive, of course, and also small and light enough to mail easily.

It had been almost three weeks since she had sent him anything, which felt like way too long. With no better idea, Maggie decided to send him more baseball cards, so she went down to Mr. Aldo's shop to buy a pack.

And there, at the candy counter, she found a perfect gift.

I'm putting something for Jay in with this letter. It's a new thing Mr. Aldo just started selling at his shop. If you flip open the top, a little piece of candy comes out.

It's called PEZ, I hope he likes it!

Six

GAME SEVEN

*T*he start of the school year always made Maggie feel a little breathless. New teacher, different kids in her class, the feeling of being a year older, which was somehow a lot stronger when she went into a new grade than it was on her birthday. She had a new white blouse with a darling round collar. And after weeks of begging, she had finally persuaded Mom to cut bangs into her hair. She couldn't pass a mirror or a window without pausing to look at her reflection; the bangs really did make her look older.

Besides that, Treecie was back from Long Island, and they had so much to talk about. They talked as fast as they could every second on the way to school and at recess and when they saw each other on the weekends, and still it seemed as if they would never get caught up.

But Maggie had hardly anything new to tell Treecie about Jim—because she hadn't received a letter from him in ages. Mr. Armstrong didn't call out to her anymore on Saturday mornings; he just shook his head as soon as he came around the corner.

One evening at bedtime, Maggie opened the lid of the shoebox where she kept Jim's letters. She took them out of their envelopes and put them on the bedspread.

Six letters from Jim, with the one note from Jay-Hey.

May 31. That was when Jim's last letter had been written. Jay's note had come in the same envelope.

And now it was the beginning of September. More than three whole months without a letter.

Why was it taking so long? Were his letters getting lost in the mail? Or was he just not writing to her anymore?

Maggie refolded the letters, put them back into their envelopes, and returned them to the shoebox. She pressed her lips together hard.

There were two possible reasons why she hadn't heard from Jim in so long. And neither was good news.

The first reason was easier to talk about.

"I mean, I thought we were friends, but maybe I'm wrong," Maggie said as she and Treecie walked home from school the next day. "Maybe to him I'm just some—some pesky little kid, but he had to be nice to me because my dad got him his job."

"What are you talking about—of *course* he likes you!" Treecie said. "If it was because of your dad, do you think he'd have spent hours and *hours* scoring games with you? Don't be ridiculous. He could have given you a—a Hershey bar or something if he just wanted to be nice!"

Maggie had to smile. Treecie, loyal and reassuring and annoyed all at the same time.

"Still, maybe it was stupid of me to keep writing to him," Maggie said. "I—I don't know why—"

"I do," Treecie said. "Baseball."

"Well, sure, but—"

"No, listen. I mean, I like baseball and I love the Dodgers and all that, but when you two talk about baseball, it's almost a whole different game. The stuff in your scorebooks—it's like some secret code or something, that nobody else could figure out. What I mean is, you talk about baseball different to him than anybody else. And you miss that."

Maggie looked at Treecie gratefully and nodded. It was true. Ever since Jim had left, she had been going to the firehouse less often. Not that she didn't like the other guys; they were her pals, especially George, and she still listened to games with them from time to time. But it wasn't the same without Jim there.

"Anyway, maybe it's not his fault," Treecie said.

"What do you mean?"

"Well, suppose he's not an ambulance guy anymore. Suppose he got transferred into some super-secret spy job, and he's not allowed to write to anyone. Or he's . . . he's behind enemy lines or—wait, I know!"

Treecie stopped walking and grabbed Maggie's arm, her eyes wide. "He's been captured! He's a prisoner-of-war, and he's being kept in some awful jail, and the—the warden's daughter is really smart, and she sneaks him extra food, and they've fallen in love, and she's figuring out a plan to help him escape!"

"C'mon, Treece, this isn't a movie," Maggie said.

Still, Treecie had said aloud what Maggie had been thinking: The second possibility was that Jim *couldn't* write to her.

He's still alive, she thought. *If he wasn't, we would know—Dad would have heard.*

Not dead, then. Hurt? Or captured?

And how could she find out?

She asked her dad first. Dad said he hadn't heard anything about Jim, so the next time Maggie passed by the firehouse, she spoke to George.

"Yeah, Maggie-o, I did hear somethin'," he said. He set down the sandwich he was holding and wiped his mouth with a paper napkin. "I mean, it wasn't me, it was his sister."

George went on to explain that Jim's sister in New Jersey had phoned to say she had received a letter. "She told me things are a little tough for him. But he— he's doin' okay, I guess." He paused for a moment, then picked up the sandwich and waved it at her. "Bologna?" he said.

Maggie shook her head.

"You sure? Aw, go on."

Maggie saw the ragged edges of the bread and the semicircle shapes of George's bites, and it didn't look the least bit appetizing. "No thanks, George."

He shrugged. "Okay," he said. "Guess that means more for me."

Maggie said goodbye and headed home.

The relief that she felt on hearing that Jim had been in touch with his sister was tangled up with other not-so-good feelings. Of course it was normal for Jim to write to his family, but she couldn't help feeling jealous of this sister she'd never met.

And if he was still writing to other people, did it mean Treecie was wrong—that Jim wasn't a real friend after all?

Maggie thought about the games they had scored together, their long conversations about baseball, the times they had taken Charky for walks in the park. She shook her head.

I know we were friends.

There was some other reason he wasn't writing to her, and she had no idea what it could be.

Good thing the Dodgers were doing so well: The 1952 season was one day of joy after another. The Bums had been in first place since the beginning of June, winning game upon game—so many that the losses hardly hurt at all.

Secretly, Maggie knew it was at least in part because of *her.*

Before the season started, Maggie had figured out how she could help the team. She would score every play of every single game that she listened to. She wouldn't miss a single pitch.

And she would pray for the Dodgers the night before each game.

Okay, so her praying hadn't worked last year, but

maybe saying prayers was like collecting something. Maggie thought of Treecie's shells.

Years ago, when Treecie had first announced that she was collecting shells, she had only three. It was not a very impressive collection, although of course Maggie didn't tell her that.

Now on a shelf in Treecie's room, there was a big pickle jar full of shells. She had found them on the beach near her uncle's farm. "I like thinking how they could have come from really far away," Treecie had said.

Maybe saying prayers was like collecting shells— maybe you had to say a whole lot of them before they added up to something. Maggie pictured her prayers as a string of words trailing upwards. Maybe she had to say a bunch more prayers before the string was long enough to reach Heaven.

So she had stuck to her plan fiercely. The praying part was easy: Bedtime prayers were a habit, automatic. The scoring part was sometimes harder: It took a lot of concentration to score pitches and set the table at the same time, especially with Mom snapping at her to put the scorebook *down* before she broke a glass.

Now it was late September, the end of the regular season. And her plan was working!

Brooklyn had won the pennant. They would play the Yankees in the World Series. Maggie could hardly wait.

Seven games. The Series went the full seven games, back and forth, up and down, wins and losses, until

Maggie felt positively seasick. The Dodgers won Games 1, 3, and 5 but lost Games 2, 4, and 6.

By unspoken agreement, Dad was never around when the games were on. He was at work during the week, of course, and for the weekend games he went to Uncle Leo's house. Maggie was grateful for his tact; she didn't think she could have stood listening to the games with him cheering for the Yankees in the same room.

Along with probably two-thirds of the school kids in Brooklyn, Joey-Mick and Maggie stayed home after lunch on the day of Game 7. It was like the whole Series smushed into one game. First the Yankees scored, then the Dodgers tied the game; in the next inning the Yankees scored another run, and the Dodgers tied it again. Two more runs for the Yankees; they were ahead, 4–2. Joey-Mick paced the room like a big cat in a small cage, *thunk*ing the ball into his glove almost constantly. Maggie swung her leg furiously and chewed her nails and twisted her hair and kept score all at the same time.

Bottom of the seventh, Yankees still ahead, 4–2. The bases were F.O.B.—"full of Brooklyns," Red Barber's famous phrase, and with two out Jackie Robinson came to the plate. Maggie made her tiny cross gesture, forefinger against her thumb.

Jackie fouled off the first two pitches. Then he swung and made contact. The sound of the bat on the ball was wrong—a weak *tock* rather than a solid *crack*.

An infield pop-up. Maggie froze, all except for her heart, which felt like it was falling somewhere south of her toes.

But Jackie was Jackie, and this was no ordinary pop-up. It went high . . . then higher . . . the pitcher and the first baseman lost it in the sun . . . the Dodgers were running like mad around the bases . . . the ball was still in the air . . . one runner scored, then two, and the third was heading for the plate with the lead run . . . Joey-Mick was hopping up and down now . . . the Dodgers would be ahead, 5-4, with only two innings left to play . . .

Then stupid Yankee second baseman Billy Martin charged across the infield and made a stupid miracle catch, his glove just inches off the ground. With that catch, something inside Maggie seemed to give up, roll over, and die. Sure enough, the Yankees went on to win the game, and the Series, and all the glory.

Maggie had been *so sure* that this would be Brooklyn's year. After the pain they had suffered last year, losing to the Giants on that awful Thomson home run, it had felt like the Dodgers flat-out *deserved* to win if there was any justice in the world. It was so unfair—the Yankees always, always, *always* won. Would it *ever* be the Bums' turn? Would she ever get to stop thinking "Wait till next year"?

Part of her wanted to kick and scream and swear and break things, but it was as if all the life had been sucked out of her. She couldn't summon the energy for even a single tear. She got up from the armchair, went up to her room, and buried her scorebook at the bottom of the closet.

It wasn't alone: the two books from last year—regular season and playoff series against the Giants—

were there, too. *I'm never going to look at them again as long as I live,* Maggie vowed silently.

At dinner, Dad was telling Mom about something that had happened at work. It had nothing to do with baseball, and Maggie thought she was listening, but in the next moment her head was down on the table and she was sobbing into her napkin.

Dad stopped talking and put down his forkful of mash—it was a Tuesday, potatoes night—which he had been waving in the air as he spoke.

"Hey," he said, in what for him was a soft voice. He reached out and touched the back of Maggie's head. "Hey there."

Maggie sobbed a little louder.

Joey-Mick spoke up. "It's the Dodgers, Dad. She's mad about the Series."

"I know, I know," Dad said. "It's okay, princess. They did great, didn't they? The full seven games. That hardly ever happens to the Yanks. You know the last team that did it?"

"Yeah, we know, Dad," Joey-Mick said angrily. "The Dodgers, in forty-seven. We lost then, too!"

"I'm just sayin'," Dad said, "that the Dodgers got nothing to be ashamed of."

Then Maggie lifted her head. "E-easy for y-you to say," she said, her words snagging on each sob, "you— you're a *Yankees fan!*" She spat out the last words like a curse, jumped up from her chair, and fled toward the stairs.

"*Margaret Olivia!*" Mom said, standing up so fast

that her chair fell backward and hit the floor with a loud thump. "You do *not* talk to your father like that—"

Maggie pounded up the stairs and slammed the bedroom door to cut off the rest of her mother's words. Now she'd really be in for it—talking back to Dad *and* slamming the door on Mom. She held her breath for a moment, listening. Dad's voice was too low for her to make out what he was saying, but he must have been telling Mom to stay cool and leave her alone, because nobody came after her. Then his voice rose a little, and she heard him say, "Son, pick up your mother's chair."

Maggie sat on the edge of her bed, trembling. She had thought she was ready for a good long cry, but her tears had dried up suddenly. She tried to swallow the dry lump in her throat, which almost made her gag.

Stupid Dodgers. How could they do this to her? She didn't feel one bit sorry for them. They had let her down, her and Joey-Mick and Mom and Treece and the guys at the firehouse . . . the whole neighborhood—the whole *city*.

Maybe she would become a Yankees fan—it would be nice to cheer for a team that won all the time. But the thought was hardly formed in her mind before she shook it off with a shudder. She could never be a Yankees fan. Or a Giants fan, either, except for cheering for Willie Mays. It was impossible—like saying she should be a dog instead of a girl.

That would be much better, come to think of it. Charky never really cared who won the games. The guys at the firehouse said he was a Dodgers fan, but that was because *they* were happy when the Dodgers won, and when they were happy, Charky was happy.

It was stupid saying that a dog was a fan of a certain team.

Maggie slammed herself back onto the bed and put the pillow over her face. Everything was stupid. Especially *her*.

All that scoring, all those times she hadn't gone to the bathroom when she needed to, so she wouldn't miss a pitch. And how many times had she prayed! One hundred fifty-four games in the season, plus the seven games of the Series—that made 161 prayers for the Dodgers. Surely enough to reach up to Heaven, and they *still* hadn't won the Series.

She took the pillow off so she could take a deep breath and swallow again. Above the bed on the wall were the two pictures, one of Willie, the other of Jim and Jay-Hey.

Jim.

He was stupid, too. Why wasn't he writing to her anymore? What was going on over there in Korea? Maggie realized that Jim had never written anything about the war in his letters. Not one single thing. Nothing about any bombs or guns or battles. How could she possibly even guess what was happening to him? And to Willie Mays too, who had been in the army for almost the entire season . . .

She glared at Jim's face in the photo for a long moment. He was smiling, and because he had been looking right into the camera's lens when the photo was snapped, it looked as though he was smiling at *her*.

Maggie felt her cheeks redden. It wasn't his fault, not really. But since he wasn't telling her anything about the war, she would just have to learn about it herself somehow.

And it wasn't Dad's fault that the Dodgers had lost.

Maggie stood up slowly, then headed back downstairs.

Dad and Mom and Joey-Mick were still at the dinner table. They stared at her as she came into the room.

Joey-Mick said, "Your turn to clear! I thought you were trying to get out of it."

"Joseph Michael, that's enough," Mom said.

Maggie looked at Dad. "I'm sorry I shouted," she mumbled. Then, "I didn't mean to slam the door" to Mom.

A brief silence. Mom nodded, then shrugged. "So," she said, "next year starts again."

Maggie tried to smile and almost managed it, but not quite. Every year was next year, and next year never came.

Seven

TERRITORY

$\mathcal{I}$t was not easy to figure out what was happening in the war.

Maggie had bought a new notebook, thinking that she would write down things about the war. She had been reading war stories in the newspaper for almost a month now. There were usually at least two articles on the front page: one about the fighting and another about the talking. The soldiers were doing the fighting, and the government people were doing the talking— endless meetings, where they tried to make a deal to end the war.

The articles about the fighting were hard enough. "U.N. troops withdraw . . . foe in possession of strategic hill . . . consolidation of position . . ." Maggie read and reread the stories, but she still couldn't "see" what was happening.

And the articles about the talking—they were downright impossible! "Repatriation of prisoners"? "Stalemate on non-aggression clause"? "Regional economic impact"? No wonder those government men couldn't agree on anything—they were too busy looking up all the words in the dictionary!

She put the paper down and picked up her notebook again. On the first spread, she had written *S.K. / U.S. / U.N.* at the top of one page, and *N.K. / COMM.* on the opposite page.

South Korea, the United States, and the United Nations against North Korea and the Communists. Those were the two teams. Well, not teams, but sides.

She looked at the two headings, then made all the letters into block letters, fatter and darker than before.

There. That was better.

But there was nothing else written on either page. No matter how much she read, she couldn't figure out what to write down.

The almost-empty pages reminded her of the times she had come running home from school in time for the last inning of a game. For those games, there were only a few plays recorded.

Maggie took a breath and sat very still for a moment.

It's because I've come in at the end of the game—I mean, the war. Well, maybe not the end, but at least in the middle. I don't have any idea what happened before, so nothing makes sense.

She nodded slowly. Even though she still didn't have the solution, at least she knew what part of the problem was: How did the war start, and what had happened between then and now?

*   *   *

"Library," Dad said. "They keep newspapers from a ways back. Why do you wanna know?"

"I need to learn about how the war got started," Maggie said. She had asked him how she could see newspapers from 1950, when the war began. "I thought maybe then I could sort of figure out what might be happening to Jim."

"Oh." Dad was quiet for a moment, started to speak, stopped. He pulled at one side of his mustache, which he often did when he was thinking.

"You'll probably need Mom's help," he said at last. "I don't think it's as easy as checking out a book."

Mom was always the one who took Maggie to the library. But it was a busy time of year: school, Treecie's birthday, Thanksgiving, Maggie's birthday, Christmas. Maggie kept asking, and finally, one day during Christmas break, Mom found the time to go with her.

The library at Grand Army Plaza was one of Maggie's favorite places. Mom had taken her there ever since she was a baby; the library had opened the same year Maggie was born. One of their regular outings, with Maggie in the baby carriage and Joey-Mick toddling alongside, had been a walk through Prospect Park to the enormous building at the north end, its entry flanked by huge columns and framed with gilded ironwork. They would walk through the big doors and pick out books and read and have a nice rest until it was time to go home again.

When Maggie was older, Mom explained to her that the library had been built to resemble a book. The entry area was the spine, and the two big wings of the building fanned out to either side, like a book that was partly open. For Maggie, that was the clincher: It was surely the most wonderful building in the world.

Even now she loved walking through those big doors, from the traffic and clamor of the busy plaza into the sudden peace of the lobby.

"Through here," Mom said and led the way to the periodicals room.

Finding the articles turned out to be a lot of work. The desk clerk helped them. First they had to look up "Korean conflict" in a big thick book that listed articles by subject. Then on little slips of paper they wrote down the dates and page numbers given in the book. They gave the slips to the clerk, who went off somewhere and brought back cardboard boxes labeled with the matching dates.

The boxes contained reels of microfilm. The clerk led them to the area where the large microfilm viewers were kept. He showed them how to wind one end of the film through the viewer's lens and onto an empty takeup reel.

Finally, Maggie pressed a switch to turn on the viewer's lamp, and there on the screen was the front page of an old newspaper. Magnified, so the almost invisible print on the film was blown up enough to read easily. It was like magic.

To get to another page, you turned a handle that moved the film along. Maggie had to keep looking back and forth from the slips of paper to the screen, reeling past pages and pages of articles that had nothing to do with the war.

The first articles she looked at were from the summer of 1950, almost three years earlier. The war had begun when she was only eight years old!

At first Maggie found it interesting to look at articles from so far back, but as she reeled through the yards and yards of microfilm, her disappointment grew. It felt like more of what she had already been doing—reading stuff about the war that she couldn't really understand.

And it certainly wasn't helping her one bit with figuring out what might be happening to Jim.

On another viewer, Mom was reeling through other articles. For a while it was quiet, the two of them reeling and reading. . . . Maggie began to get dizzy from the words sliding by in front of her eyes.

Then Mom made a little clicking noise with her tongue. "Come here and have a look now," she said.

Maggie scooted her chair over so she could look at the screen of Mom's viewer.

"Land," Mom said. "War is about land, territory. One side trying to control more than the other. Before World War II, Germany was taking over Europe a wee bit at a time, and the fighting was all about trying to get it back from them."

On the viewer was a map of Korea. Part of it was shaded with diagonal lines.

"See those lines?" Mom said. "That's showing you how much territory one side has. Now then. You'll be needing maps like this right from the beginning of the war. Here, give us a piece of paper."

Mom held the sheet of paper right up to the

screen. Very lightly, she traced the outline of Korea and then the diagonal lines.

"April 1951," she said. "You'll be going back further and then forward again."

Instead of spooling randomly for articles about the war, Maggie was now looking for something specific. It made the search go much more quickly.

I'm on a treasure hunt, she thought. *And the treasure is maps.*

By the time they left the library three long hours later, Maggie had torn out the first two pages of her notebook and started over. On the way home she made plans: She would need to draw over the light tracings to make them darker, add captions, make more copies of the maps. . . .

As soon as they got home, Maggie went right to the dining table and started working.

Joey-Mick plopped himself down next to her, glove on one hand, ball in the other. *Thunk—thunk—* "Whatcha doin'?"—*thunk—thunk.*

"What's it look like I'm doing?"

He watched her for a few moments, then frowned. "We didn't have no project like that in fifth grade."

"It's not for school."

The *thunk*ing stopped. "It's *not*? What's it for, then?"

"It's not for anything. I mean, it's just for me. I'm trying to learn more about the war."

"We're learning about World War II right now.

I'd like to have been one of them parachute-jumpers. They got dropped behind the enemy lines, and then they had to do some special mission and get back to the other side. Without getting caught by the Nazis."

Maggie angled the sheet of paper in front of her toward him, so he could see it better. "See those diagonal lines there? That's the enemy. The Communists. The plain space, that's South Korea and the U.S."

Joey-Mick looked at the map. "It's almost exactly half and half."

"On that one, yeah. But"—she sorted through the pile of maps she had traced at the library—"look at this one. And this one here."

"Wow," he said. "That musta been a *lot* of fighting."

Maggie began working again. She needed to make copies of the outline of Korea. Her plan was to make a new map at least once a month, or whenever there was a change in territory.

Joey-Mick plunked the ball one last time. Then he took off the glove, the ball safe in its pocket, and put it on the table. "Want some help?" he asked. He picked up another pencil and started tracing, too.

The maps took a whole week of work, but it was worth it in the end. Maggie paged through her notebook several times after she finished, admiring the result. Not only had she redrawn the traced maps, but she had also added captions using what she had learned from reading all those articles.

MAPS OF THE KOREAN WAR
by Margaret Olivia Fortini

Map 1

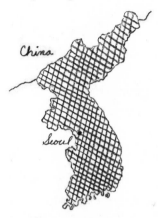

1910–1945: Korea is all one country, but it's been taken over by Japan.

Map 2

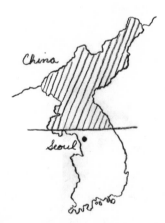

1945: Japan loses World War II and has to leave Korea. Both Russia and the U.S. want Korea to be on their side. So they make a deal: The U.S. gets to help the government in the south of the country, and Russia gets to help the north. They make a line across the middle of the country.

Map 3

China

Seoul

June–Sept. 1950: The Communists in the north part of Korea want to control the south part, too, so they send soldiers to try to take over.

The south is caught by surprise—nobody there expected the invasion. By August, the Commies take over most of the country, including Seoul, the capital. They push all the way through until the only part they haven't taken over is a tiny corner in the south.

Map 4

Sept.–Nov. 1950: President Truman asks the United Nations to send troops to Korea to help the southern side. U.S. and U.N. soldiers land in Korea and start fighting back.

By November, the south is winning! They get control of Seoul again, and they push the enemy almost all the way back—almost to the border with China!

Map 5

Nov. 1950–Jan. 1951: China sends troops to help the north side. With all those Chinese Commies to help, the north starts taking back the territory they lost. They get control of Seoul again and keep pushing south.

Map 6

Jan.–June 1951: The U.S. and other countries send more soldiers to help. They stop the attack and push north again, but not as far this time—only to the middle of the country. But at least they get Seoul back, hurrah!

Map 7

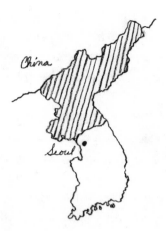

June–Sept. 1951: Battles along the line in the middle.

Maggie couldn't get over the difference between maps 3 and 4. In just three months, too. That was what had impressed Joey-Mick when she showed it to him.

A lot of fighting, he had said.

Maps 8, 9, and 10 covered the rest of 1951 and all of 1952. They looked just like map 7. According to the articles, there had been many battles along the dividing line during that time. But neither side had made any real gains in territory.

Maggie sat there, thinking hard. Then she rose and took the book of maps into her bedroom.

She looked at the photo of Jim and Jay-Hey on her wall.

Jim was working with the ambulance guys. *So he's near the fighting. Maybe even* in *the fighting sometimes. Because that's what the ambulance guys would do—*

they'd go to where the fighting was and pick up the sol-diers who've been shot by the Commies and take them somewhere else. Where doctors could help them.

And if Jim's camp was near the front lines, then that was where Jay lived.

Maggie traced the line between the two areas of territory on the last map. It was, as Joey-Mick had pointed out, almost exactly in the middle of the country.

Jay lives somewhere near this line. Where there's been more fighting than anywhere else.

She tried to imagine it. Bursts of gunfire. Grenades exploding. Airplanes dropping bombs.

Right around your house.

Maggie got a picture in her head. Jay sitting quiet-ly, studying the baseball cards she had sent him. And then a huge *BOOM!* and the house shaking like crazy and Jay diving to the floor and lying there curled up in a little ball, the cards scattered around him. . . .

Was that what it was like? Being really scared almost every minute all day long?

Now she had two reasons for wanting the war to end: So Jim could come home, and so Jay wouldn't have to be scared all the time.

Eight

POINTS

*M*aggie understood a whole lot more about the war now. But that didn't magically produce a letter from Jim.

She had stopped asking Dad if he had heard any news about Jim. The answer was always the same: No—but he would tell her as soon as he heard. Maggie was sick of asking, and she was sure that Dad was just as sick of giving the same answer every time.

She continued to write to Jim—not as often as before, but she had been writing to him for so long now that it felt like it would be wrong to stop.

April 14, 1953

Dear Jim,

Opening Day—FINALLY! Good news for both of us: The Dodgers beat the Pirates 8–5 and the Giants beat the Phillies 4–1. . . .

May 31, 1953

Dear Jim,

I got something great to write to you about today. During the World Series last year (that's not the great part, in fact I HATE thinking about it) Gil Hodges didn't get a single hit, he went 0 for 21. And he started off this year the same way—he was hitting just AWFUL, and he even got BENCHED and he hasn't been benched in AGES.

So in the paper I read about how people were all worried about him—they were writing him letters and sending him good-luck charms and everything. There was even a priest who asked for prayers for him.

Anyway, then Treecie told me that her mom told her what happened at knitting circle. The ladies always end knitting circle with a prayer, and my mom asked everyone to pray for Gil Hodges! She must have read that same article, and I never asked her but I bet he's her favorite player.

And this is the best part—it WORKED. Yesterday the Dodgers beat the Pirates 4–1, and Gil Hodges hit TWO home runs. Isn't that amazing?

June 27, 1953

Dear Jim,

In case you don't know already: Willie Mays is FINE. My dad found out from a magazine—Willie never went overseas at all. He said he would have gone to Korea but they never asked him to. And the best part is, his job in the Army is to play base-ball! Maybe you know this already, that the Army has a baseball team that goes around playing games so the soldiers can watch. That's what Willie does. Maybe you'll get to see him!

As the weeks went by, Maggie continued to read the newspaper faithfully, both the baseball news and articles about the war. Once in a while, she drew a new map in her war notebook, but every single one of them was identical to the one before it, and all of them looked like map 7, from June 1951.

Two whole years . . . and the line hadn't budged.

One afternoon as she finished reading yet another article about the war, Maggie noticed an item on the same page of the paper:

Casualties from New York

And there was a long list of names.

Killed in action. Died of wounds. Wounded.

Maggie gasped. How was it that she had never seen a list like this before? Maybe it was because the print was so tiny—the smallest print on the whole page. Almost as though the newspaper was trying to hide it.

Killed in action. . . . What if Jim's name was on that list ages ago—and I missed it?

The moment of panic subsided quickly: She reminded herself again that if Jim had been killed, Dad would have told her about it.

Just then there was a knock at the door, and she heard Treecie's voice. "Hi, Mrs. Fortini. Maggie home?"

Treecie rushed up the stairs and into the room. "Look!" she said and held out an envelope.

A letter from Jim?

Maggie took the envelope from Treecie. It was addressed to people she didn't know—Christopher and Claire Moran—and it wasn't Jim's handwriting.

"What is this?" she demanded.

Treecie plopped down on the bed, blew out her breath, and caught it again. "It's friends of my mom's. Their son, his name is Carl, he's in Korea. Mrs. Moran came over today and brought this letter to show my mom, and I heard her read it out loud and I asked if I could borrow it to show you, and she let me take it but I have to bring it right back."

Maggie read:

> *June 1, 1953*
>
> *Dear Mom and Dad,*
>
> *You asked if I'd be home for Mom's birthday. Here's how it works: You need 36 points to go home, you get 3 points for every month in the rear and 4 points if you're on the front lines. We moved to the front in October but the Army has its little tricks, if you don't have a full month at the front you*

only get 3 points so we were three days short
of the full month when they moved us. That
means I got 14 points so far, 3 points for Feb.
and Mar. and 4 points for Apr and May.
That's almost halfway there already, only
22 points to go, if I'm on the front the whole
time that means only 6 months more,
maybe I'll make it home in time. . . .

Maggie stopped reading, her eyes wide.

"Treece . . ."

"I know, I know!"

They looked at each other, and Maggie knew they were both thinking the same thing.

Jim had left in January 1952. He didn't get to Korea until February, or maybe even March. And he probably didn't get to count four points for each month because he wasn't on the front lines the whole time— he'd be driving the ambulance back and forth between the front lines and the army hospitals in the rear. So that meant three points for each month. It was almost the end of June now, so if she started counting from March of last year, that meant 15 months. . . .

Jim should have 45 points by now! He would have had 36 points three months ago. Why wasn't he home?

Maggie jumped to her feet. She called over her shoulder as she went out the door. "Mom, going to the firehouse for just a minute, be right back!"

Treecie was right behind her as she raced down the street. "Why the firehouse?" she asked.

"You'll see," Maggie panted.

They ran all the way, Charky meeting them as usual and barking as he galloped alongside them. "Shh, shh, it's okay, Charks," Maggie said and patted him on the head as she slowed and walked the last few steps.

The bay doors were open, but the guys weren't out front. Maggie peered past the engines and saw that the door to the back room was open. "Hello?" she called.

"Come on in, Maggie-o," George answered. He was tipping back in his chair so he could lean out and see them. "Hey, Treecie."

The girls walked between the two trucks. George and the other guys, Vince and Terry and Charlie, were playing cards. An electric fan was on, doing little more than blowing the hot air around the room.

"Hi, George. Hi, everyone," Maggie said from the doorway. Then she plunged right in, still a little breathless from her run. "George—I just came to ask— remember you told me that one time about when Jim's sister called and she'd gotten a letter from him—well, I was wondering, did she call again?"

She took a breath and went on. "I mean, has she gotten any more letters from him, and did she say how he's doing? And maybe when he'll be coming home? It's been a while and I figured somebody must have heard from him since then—" She stopped, suddenly aware of how fast she was talking.

"Because we just found out about the points, see, and he should have enough to come home by now," Treecie added. Which wasn't terribly helpful, Maggie thought, if you didn't know what she was talking about.

George was sitting very still, looking down at the cards in his hand. Maggie looked from him to Terry, who was suddenly busy adjusting a suspender strap.

The silence in the room made the air seem thicker somehow. Maggie drew in a deep breath and felt as though she could hear it all the way down to her lungs.

"George?" she said.

"Uh, yeah." George closed the fan of his cards and tapped the stack on the tabletop a few times. Finally, he looked up at her. "Maggie-o, I don't know how much I oughta say, and anyways I don't know much. I don't wanna make any trouble."

Maggie stared at him. Trouble? What kind of trouble?

George sighed. "Listen, maybe he's gonna be mad at me for this, but I don't know what else to do. What you asked me just now—you go on home and ask Teeny Joe. You tell him it's my fault if you want."

His fault? His fault for doing what? And who was going to be mad? Maggie was so utterly bewildered that she blinked twice hard, as if clearing her vision might help.

"Who? Who's going to be mad?" Treecie asked right out.

George glanced at her, then shook his head. "Maggie, you talk to your dad, okay?" Then he fanned out his cards again. "You gonna play, or what?" he growled at Charlie.

"Yeah, yeah," Charlie said.

It was clear that they had been dismissed.

"C'mon, Maggie," Treecie said.

They turned and walked slowly out of the fire-house.

Treecie went home to deliver the letter safely back to Mrs. Moran. Maggie sat down on the front stoop and watched and waited. She knew it was Dad as soon as he turned the corner; she couldn't see his face clearly at this distance, but she could tell by the way he limped.

Maggie jumped up and ran to meet him. Dad looked at her and smiled, but it was a quiet smile, not his usual big open grin. Which meant that he had stopped by the firehouse and had already talked to George.

"Hey, Maggie-o," he said.

She fell in step beside him. They were both silent for half a block, until Maggie couldn't stand it any longer.

"Dad?" she said.

They walked the rest of the way to the house. Dad sat down on the front stoop and nodded at the space next to him. Maggie sat, too, and waited.

"I'm sorry, Maggie-o," he said at last. "About a bunch of things."

He sighed and pulled at his mustache. "I didn't mean to keep stuff from you. I thought I was just tak-ing the time to decide what to tell you, and then I was hoping that—that things would get better and I could give you some good news, and then—well, before I knew it, a lotta weeks had passed and it got easier not to tell you anything. And the whole time I was still hopin' for good news." He raised his head and looked at her. "I almost told you a million times, but I could never—I dunno, I couldn't seem to find the right time. So that's the first thing I'm sorry for."

"Okay." She didn't know what else to say.

He went on. "Remember when George told you that Jim's sister had called? The truth of it is, it was me she called. And I told George and the guys what she told me, but I asked them not to say much of anything to you until . . . until I could figure what you should know. They—they sorta fibbed, I guess, but it was because I asked them to. I'm sorry about that, too."

Maggie twisted away from him, so she could turn and look at him straight on. "Dad, please just tell me."

His answer came slowly. "What his sister said was, there was a big battle. And Jim was with the ambulance guys—you know that, right? So there's this battle, and he works like a crazy man to take care of as many injured people as he can. All day and all night and most of the next day, without taking a single break."

Maggie pictured Jim helping carry a stretcher, but even as the image popped into her head, she knew it was wrong. For one thing, she imagined him in his fireman kit. That wasn't right; he would have been wearing a soldier's uniform. And his face all sooty, like after a fire. But maybe that was okay; maybe you got sooty in the middle of a battle too, all those guns and grenades and bombs going off around you.

"Finally, his officer told him to get some rest. So Jim got into his bunk and then . . . well, he just sorta stayed there."

"What do you mean?'

Her father sighed again. "He didn't get up. Not for a meal, not for his next shift on duty. His buddies tried everything they could think of to get him out of bed, finally called in their officer, and the guy even threatened Jim with jail time. But nothing happened. He was kinda, like, frozen."

"Frozen?" From the newspaper articles, Maggie had learned that it was really cold in Korea in the winter, much colder than in Brooklyn.

"Well, no, I don't mean frozen like cold. I mean, he didn't move, didn't say a word, didn't even look at anyone. Just sort of stared at nothin' the whole time."

"But what was wrong with him? Was he hurt?"

Dad shook his head. "Not physically. Not anything they could find. He was in the hospital in Japan for a while, and then in Seattle, and finally he ended up in Washington, D.C. That's where he's been for the past year."

Maggie's mouth dropped open. "But—but my letters! I've been sending them to Korea. . . ."

All those letters, and he hadn't even gotten them?

Dad patted her arm. "Now, Maggie-o, I seen you writing all them letters, and keeping score of the Giants' games for him, and those cookies—don't you think I'd make sure they got to where they were supposed to?"

Maggie sat there thinking hard. Her letter-mailing

routine: She would address the envelope, then leave it on the little table in the hall . . . and Dad would pick it up in the morning on his way out the door for work.

He was the one who would put a stamp on it and mail it.

"So you . . ."

He nodded. "I kept track the whole time, where he was. Through his sister, her name's Carol, and I made sure to send 'em to the right place. And she mentioned your letters, said what a great girl you are, to write to him so regular like that. She told me she reads 'em aloud to him, every one of 'em.

"He's up out of the wheelchair now, some of the time, walking a little, feeding himself . . . but he still hasn't said a single word to anyone," Dad went on. "Anyway, they don't think there's anything more they can do for him at the hospital, so they're sending him home."

"Home?" Maggie echoed. She thought of her plans for a grand welcome-home party. Now it didn't seem like there was much to celebrate. . . .

"To Carol's," Dad said. "There's nowhere else for him to go—he was living on his own here in town, but there's still too many things he can't do for himself."

"Can we go see him?"

"Not right away, Maggie-o. It'll be a big change for him. We gotta wait and see how he does. Carol's hoping it'll help—she's got two boys, they're nuts about him, she thinks being around them might do him some good. If he gets better some . . . then we'll see.

"It's been hard on Carol too. She's been making the

trip to D.C. every month to visit him. I got the guys to take up a collection, sent her money to help out, but I sure wish there was something more we could do."

"I have three dollars and twenty-six cents," Maggie said immediately. "I can send that, I know it isn't much, but—"

Dad smiled at her. "You just keep writing to him. That's the best thing you can do, and it's a lot more than you think." He paused, then added, "You might say a prayer for him, too."

He elbowed her gently. "C'mon, let's go eat."

"I'll—I'll be in in a minute, okay?" she said.

He hesitated a moment, then nodded. "Suit yourself. Don't be too long, princess." He rubbed his bad knee, then heaved himself to his feet.

Maggie heard the door close. She bent her head down and squeezed her eyes shut, as if she might somehow be able to block the wave of hot shame rising inside her.

All those months she had been praying for the Dodgers—when she should have been praying for Jim.

Why hadn't she started praying for him right when the letters stopped coming? For that matter, she could have prayed for him the minute he went into the army! She *knew* people did that—she had heard them ask for intercessions in church—she could have asked for one for Jim—why hadn't she thought of it?

Maggie wasn't crying, but she found herself taking quick gasps of air that seemed to catch in her throat. She had been so selfish, praying for the Dodgers—for something *she* wanted. If she had prayed to God to keep Jim safe, maybe this wouldn't have happened, maybe he would have been fine and home months ago. . . .

If any of it, even a little tiny crumb, was her fault, she would have to make up for it somehow.

Maggie opened her eyes, blinked a few times, and glanced up and down the street. Nobody around. She crossed herself, then laced her fingers together and brought her clasped hands to her face as she breathed out the words.

"Dear God, please bless Mom and Dad and Joey-Mick and me and all our friends and relations and the most abandoned souls in Purgatory. And especially Jim. Amen."

Nine

NOT ENOUGH

*I*n bed that night, Maggie prayed again. Then she thought about her letters, which had never gotten to Korea after all. She realized now that it had been important to her, the idea that they were going somewhere so far away. It was disappointing to think that they had stayed right here in the U.S.

And what had happened to the things she had sent to Jay—the comic books, the Pez candy? It would be nice if Jim's sister had maybe sent them on to him, but that was probably too much to expect. More disappointment: Maybe he never got any of it, except for those first cards.

Jim, sick all this time, not talking to anyone for months now. And Dad had known, and hadn't told her. Who else had known—everyone but her? But Maggie found that she couldn't really be mad at Dad for not telling her sooner. Because, in a way, what difference did it make? Jim wasn't here, so she wrote letters to him: It would have been the same even if she had known earlier what she knew now.

No, that wasn't quite right. One thing would have been different: She wouldn't have been waiting all this time for him to write back.

But maybe . . . maybe if she had known he wouldn't be writing back, she would have felt differently. Maggie realized then that every time she had sat down to write Jim a letter, she had thought something like, *THIS is the one he'll write back to.* If she had known about him being sick, she might not have written to him nearly as often. She might have stopped writing entirely.

Sure enough, writing to him from then on felt different. Awkward.

July 13, 1953

Dear Jim,

My dad told me about what happened to you. I was glad to hear that you're getting out of the hospital! I hope you'll be feeling better really soon.

I don't know if I should still write to you about baseball stuff. I guess your sister or her family could tell you the scores, or maybe you're even listening to the games yourself. But you can just let me know if you don't want me to write to you about baseball anymore.

The Giants beat the Dodgers two out of three in their last series. The Dodgers are still in first place, just barely—1½ games ahead of the Braves. 6½ ahead of the Giants, who are in fifth place, sorry. But the Giants swept the Phillies last week, including both games of a doubleheader, so they've been playing good lately, in fact before the Dodgers beat them yesterday they won eight in a row, so that's good news for you!

Not much happening around here lately—no games either, three days off for the All-Star game tomorrow. I hope you feel good enough to come visit soon. I bet Charky will remember you!

Your friend Maggie

July 28, 1953

TO JIM STOP I GUESS YOU HEARD THE NEWS BY NOW STOP CEASE-FIRE IN KOREA YESTERDAY STOP THE WAR IS OVER STOP WHAT GREAT NEWS STOP BIG QUESTION WILL WILLIE COME HOME IN TIME TO PLAY THE REST OF THE SEASON STOP

(In case you're wondering, I wanted to make this look like a telegram. I never got a telegram or sent one either but I always wanted to.)

Your friend Maggie

The newspaper printed a map of the way Korea

would be divided, into communist North Korea and democratic South Korea. Maggie traced the map to add it to her war notebook.

Then she added a caption:

July 1953: Cease-fire! The war is over!

Maggie frowned and turned back a few pages until she found what she was looking for. Map 7, from the summer of 1951.

The new map looked almost exactly like it. The line dividing the two sides was in the same place.

More than two long years of fighting. . . Thousands and thousands of soldiers on both sides dead, thousands more hurt, like Jim.

And in all that time, the line hadn't moved, hadn't budged.

Maggie looked carefully at her work. The exclamation points . . . they looked too—too happy, or something. She erased them and put periods instead:

July 1953: Cease-fire. The war is over.

Maggie could still remember the parade when World War II ended, even though she had been only three and a half. Dad wasn't with them that day; he was at work, helping with crowd control, and he wouldn't let his family watch from the street, of course—too many people. So they had gone to Uncle Leo's place in Manhattan and watched the parade from the roof. What had most impressed Maggie was all the confetti and ticker tape falling from the sky, and after the parade was over, she and Joey-Mick went down to the street and picked up handfuls and threw them into the air to watch them fall again.

She wondered if there would be another parade in New Jersey, and if Jim would be well enough to march in it. Maybe they could even go to that parade; she could stand at the curb and wave a little American flag and cheer for Jim when he marched by.

When she asked Dad about it, he fiddled with his mustache. "There's always big crowds at a parade," he said. "But I guess it's not the same as indoors. I dunno, I'll think about it. Doesn't matter this time anyway. There isn't gonna be any parade."

"What do you mean, no parade?"

Dad shook his head. "They're sayin' it wasn't ever a war."

Maggie stared at him in disbelief.

He must have seen the expression on her face, because his next words were gentle. "We never declared war on North Korea," he said. "Not officially. Congress has to do that, and they never did. I think they called it a 'police action'—whatever that means. So we can't even really say, 'The war is over,' because it wasn't a war."

Maggie thought of Jim. She felt a little knot of fury tighten inside her. She knew it wasn't right to think that she was smarter than all the congressmen in the whole U.S. of A., but she couldn't help herself: It had been a war, all right, no matter what the stupid Congress said.

In the fall, the Dodgers won the National League pennant again, a whopping thirteen games ahead of the second-place Milwaukee Braves. Never in Maggie's years as a fan had one team so thoroughly dominated the league. Brooklyn had gone into first place at the end of June and never left. They had the pennant locked up a full two weeks before the season ended. The Giants ended up in fifth place; Willie Mays didn't come home to finish the season with them. Maggie read in the paper that even though the war was over, he had to complete his two full years in the military because he hadn't spent any time overseas.

Despite the Dodgers' remarkable play all season, she tried hard to smother her hopes for the World Series. For one thing, they would be playing the Yankees again. For another, she decided that it would be better to expect the Dodgers to lose and not be disappointed if they did, and that way, if they happened to win, it would be a terrific surprise.

At least, that was what she kept telling herself.

Then Maggie read in the newspaper that radio announcer Red Barber had quit his job over a salary dispute. A guy named Vin Scully would be calling all of the World Series games. Even though Maggie knew that she wouldn't be hearing Red when she turned on the radio for Game 1, it was a jolt when she heard Mr. Scully instead. She hadn't realized how much Red's voice had become part of the game for her, and the change seemed like a bad omen for the Dodgers.

The big moment happened in Game 6. The Dodgers were down three games to two; they had to win this one to stay alive in the Series. Maggie listened to the game at home. With Brooklyn behind, 3–1, in the top of the ninth, her hopes were like a tiny flame trying to burn through wet wood—down to a final, feeble flicker, choking and gasping on thick smoke. Any moment now and she would be waiting till next year *again*. . . .

Then a small miracle occurred: Carl Furillo hit a two-run homer! The game was tied! If they could hang on in the bottom of the ninth, the game would go into extra innings—they would have a chance to win it and go on to play the seventh game.

Please, please, please . . . Maggie made the sign of the cross on her thumb.

But in the bottom of the inning, the Yanks' Billy Martin got a clutch single to drive in a run and win the game, 4–3.

Not just the game, but the Series title.

For the Yankees.

Again.

"Billy Martin!" Maggie cried out. "It's always stupid Billy Martin!" At that moment she hated him—hated him so much that she realized she had never really hated anyone before in her whole life. "He's always up at bat or all over the field or—or *something*. It's like there's twelve of him!"

She stomped up to her bedroom, jerked open the closet door, and threw the scorebook onto the floor in the corner. There was quite a pile there now: the 1951 season, another book for the playoffs that year, then 1952. And now this one.

It was the worst loss ever, even more crushing than the year before. Maggie wasn't quite sure why. Was it because she had tried so hard not to hope for too much that she had ended up hoping even more?

Maybe it was because the Dodgers had played so well all season, or because pitcher Carl Erskine had been so brilliant in the third game, setting a Series record by striking out *fourteen* Yankees. Maybe because it simply *had* to be Brooklyn's turn this time.

Or because Jim was back, but not really.

Throughout the fall, Maggie pestered Dad for news about Jim. She knew that there were regular phone calls between him and Jim's sister, and she wanted to be absolutely sure she didn't miss anything.

"If there was anything new, I'd tell you," Dad kept saying. "Carol says he's still the same."

And Maggie would say, "Okay, Dad, thanks." But she couldn't forget that he hadn't told her the truth before, and part of her didn't quite trust him. No, that wasn't true: She trusted Dad more than any other human being on the planet. But she thought it was possible that he might sort of "delay" telling her the truth again if it was bad news.

The weather grew colder. Brooklyn had its usual amount of snow that winter: flakes and flurries here and there, with one good storm that left enough snow on the ground to go sledding in the park. Maggie had outgrown her winter coat and was delighted with her new one; it was the exact color she thought of when she thought of the word "blue."

The guys went out on calls—house fires, sometimes shops or restaurants, and once a warehouse. They came back safely every time. Maggie made the sign of the cross on her thumb whenever she was at the firehouse on their return.

Which was less and less often these days. She was busier than ever with homework, as the teachers prepared the class for next year's move up to junior high. One nice surprise: the highest grade in her math class for the percentages unit, which was a breeze after all the hours she had spent calculating batting averages.

But still no word from Jim.

Nothing.

He wasn't getting better.

The letters weren't enough. And it didn't look as though her prayers were helping, either.

Ten

THE OLD SOCK

1954

*O*n a cold January afternoon, Maggie sat in the green armchair, counting the bills for what was probably the twentieth time.

"What are you gonna do with it?" Joey-Mick asked.

It was her confirmation money, seventeen dollars altogether. Five each from Uncle Pat and Uncle Leo, three from Treecie's parents, and four from the firehouse guys. Treecie had gotten even more, twenty-four dollars—she had more aunts and uncles than Maggie did.

Just as they planned, the girls had taken each other's names. On the day itself they had gone around calling each other by all four names, and "Margaret Olivia Theresa Fortini" was such a mouthful that every time Treecie said it, they both had giggle fits.

Maggie riffled the bills, then restacked them so the George Washingtons were all facing the same way.

Joey-Mick prodded her. "C'mon, you must have some idea."

"I don't know yet," Maggie said.

"I can't believe you don't got a plan," Joey-Mick said. "I had it planned out for *ages* before my confirmation." His voice cracked in midsentence, finishing much lower than it started, as if it wanted to be deep and manly but wasn't quite sure how. That happened often these days. Maggie giggled. Joey-Mick shrugged and couldn't help grinning a little himself.

Joey-Mick had been confirmed just before his thirteenth birthday a year and a half ago. The day after the service, he had taken down the magazine ad on his wall. It had been there for months: a full-page ad for the top-of-the-line Wilson fielder's glove, $19.95. The kind the big-leaguers used. He had folded the page carefully around his wad of bills, and Dad had taken him downtown.

Joey-Mick could have gotten a glove for a lot less. Eight dollars, or twelve—that was what most of the neighborhood boys paid for a glove, those who could afford one. But Joey-Mick knew what he wanted. "They don't let you get confirmed more than once," he had said. "I'm never gonna have this kind of dough again— I need to get me a glove that's gonna last forever."

He had done just that. The glove had seemed clownishly big at first, stiff with newness, but with use and several applications of neat's-foot oil, it mellowed, and Joey-Mick grew to fit it. Now it was like part of his body, on his hand that very moment as he *thunk*ed a ball into the pocket again and again.

Maggie knew that Treecie had a plan, too. She was saving her money to buy a camera. Treecie was not happy with her handed-down Brownie; she had her heart set on a Rolleiflex, a fancy German camera. The kind used by the famous photographer Margaret Bourke-White, Treecie's hero.

According to Treecie, Miss Bourke-White had taken photos all over the world, even in combat during World War II. Treecie also told Maggie that a photo taken by Miss Bourke-White had been chosen for the cover of the very first issue of *Life* magazine.

Everyone knew *Life,* of course. Mr. Armstrong brought it in the mail once a week. Treecie's family got *Life,* too; the girls often phoned each other when the magazine arrived, to talk about the interesting pictures.

"All those men photographers out there, and they picked *her* photo," Treecie had gloated.

Maggie didn't know how much a Rolleiflex cost, but she was sure it was a terrifying amount. It would take Treecie a long time to save up enough.

Thunk—thunk—

Joey-Mick, plunking the ball into his glove. And here it was the middle of January, with baseball season too far away to even be thinking about.

Maggie stared at the ball as it went back and forth ceaselessly. *Baseball season . . . the Dodgers playing again . . . the Giants . . . Willie Mays . . . Jim . . . Jim loves baseball . . .*

"I have an idea," Maggie whispered, so quietly that Joey-Mick didn't hear.

It was a good idea. Maybe even a *great* idea.

Seeing a Giants game would surely make Jim feel

better! She could take him to a game! And why not a game against the Dodgers at Ebbets Field?

Maybe Dad would say yes, because it's for Jim. Especially if I paid for it.

In the top drawer of her bureau, in an old sock—a little-girl sock, with pink lace around the cuff—Maggie had three dollars more. With her confirmation money, that made twenty dollars total. A ticket to a Dodgers game cost around two dollars. Not for box seats closest to the field—those were more expensive—but for seats in the grandstand.

I've got enough to take ten people! Jim, and Mom and Dad and Joey-Mick. And Treecie, of course, and me. That's only six, so I'd have plenty of money left over. . . .

Maggie folded down a corner of the bill on top of the stack, then unfolded it and began rolling the little point between her thumb and forefinger, thinking hard.

But maybe Jim would want his family with him. So his sister would come, too. And she has two kids, and her husband. . . .

It was getting complicated. Maggie took the money up to her bedroom and put it carefully into the old sock. Then she got out her scoring notebook and turned to a blank page at the back.

Seated on her bed, she wrote the word "People" at the top of the page. Then a list:

> JIM
> Dad, Mom, Joey-Mick
> me

Carol (Jim's sister)
Carol's two kids and husband?
Treecie
George?

That was eleven altogether. Maggie doodled a tiny baseball diamond on one corner of the page while she thought.

Tickets alone wouldn't be enough. She would need bus fare for everyone, and it would be nice if she could buy snacks at the game—hot dogs, maybe, or at least peanuts. *Thirty dollars ought to do it. I'd need ten dollars more.*

Her allowance was now twenty-five cents a week, which meant twenty cents was left after she put a nickel in the church plate. If she saved every cent—if she didn't spend a single penny on anything—it would take her fifty weeks to save ten dollars.

Fifty weeks was too long.

Okay, so no snacks. If I say just tickets and bus fare, then I wouldn't need thirty—twenty-five dollars would be enough.

Five dollars more. Twenty-five weeks instead of fifty.

She jumped up from the bed and went downstairs to look at the kitchen calendar. It was the third week of January. Maggie counted, flipping the pages. She lost track once and had to start over again. This time she counted out loud.

"Twenty-two, twenty-three, twenty-four . . ."

In twenty-five weeks it would be the middle of July.

She could do it: There would still be plenty of games left in the season.

The calendar hung a little crookedly now. Maggie straightened it, and straightened her shoulders, too. July seemed awfully far away—a long time to have to save every bit of her allowance.

And saving the money would be the easy part.

That Saturday Dad gave Maggie two dimes and a nickel, as usual. The nickel would go into the church offering plate on Sunday. The dimes were for saving. Maggie was glad it was dimes. Of all the coins, they jingled the best.

Maggie took the dollar bills out of the sock and stacked them with her confirmation money. She held the sock's top ribbing wide open. With her other hand she dropped in a dime. She did the same with the second dime, which landed with a sweet clink on its cousin. Then she gave the sock a shake to hear the jingle.

Two thin little dimes. It felt like it would be forever before she had enough.

In the afternoon she passed by Mr. Aldo's shop. Through the window she could see the jars of candy on the counter. Licorice sticks, her favorite. *I could go home and get a dime. Just one, not both of them.*

But an instant later she scolded herself: *Margaret Olivia Theresa Fortini, you will not spend that dime.*

Maggie was shaken and a little ashamed at how easily she had been tempted to cheat. She decided not to tell anyone about the plan—not Treecie, not Joey-Mick, not Mom. What if she couldn't do it? What if she told people and then didn't manage to save the money? Then she would have everyone else's disappointment to face on top of her own. No, better to keep it a secret, and that way it would be a surprise, too. As she hurried home, she resolved to try not to walk past Mr. Aldo's or the drugstore if she could help it.

But she did share her plan, just once. With Charky. She told him all about it on one of their walks.

"I can do this, Charks," she said. He barked in complete agreement, and she gave him a big hug.

The baseball season began in mid-April with a two-game series against the Giants in the Polo Grounds. The Dodgers lost the first game and won the second. And the next several weeks were sheer craziness—not just for the Dodgers and Giants. The Phillies and the Cardinals and the Braves were right in there too, all battling for the top spot and so close together that a team could go from first place to fourth in just a few games.

Vin Scully was now Brooklyn's regular radio announcer, which Maggie felt was a personal insult to both her and Red Barber. She missed Red's gentlemanly southern drawl and the familiar expressions she had heard so often: "can of corn" for an easy fly ball, "sittin' in the catbird seat" when the team was playing well. After about a month, Maggie finally gave up hope that Red would ever return, and she even had to admit that while Mr. Scully's broadcasts could never be the same as Red's, he was doing a fine job.

The Dodgers spent two weeks of June in first place,

but in the middle of the month they were overtaken by the Giants. The Bums seemed to play well only in streaks—winning five in a row, then losing the next four, winning four, then losing three. Maggie had begun making a single diagonal line from corner to corner across the entire spread of her scorebook whenever Brooklyn lost. That way, when she wanted to refer to an earlier game, she could see at a glance whether they had won or not. And slashing that line across the pages seemed like a perfect fit for her mood after a loss.

Willie Mays was back with the Giants, and having an unbelievable year—batting well over .300, hitting homers and driving in runs as if he was trying to catch up on the hundreds of games he had missed while in the army. Maggie started a special page in her scoring notebook to keep track of his statistics.

It was great to have Willie playing again . . . but it also reminded her that Jim hadn't yet returned to his old job.

Maggie could hardly believe it. She had to say it aloud to herself: "The end of July." And then, "I did it."

All those weeks and weeks turning into months and months, and now, at last, the sock in her drawer held enough dimes. After supper one evening she sat on her bed, held the sock out at arm's length, and gave it a shake. The weight of the dimes stretched the sock out in a very satisfying way, and the jingle sounded nice and crowded.

But Maggie was pleased with herself for only a few

moments. She thought about the next part of her plan: It would either go ahead or be stopped dead in its tracks *now*.

The family was in the living room, Mom knitting, Dad and Joey-Mick talking about baseball. Maggie walked in carrying the bills in one hand and the sock in the other. She put them down on the coffee table.

"Everybody," she said. Her voice came out high, almost squeaky. She cleared her throat. "I got something I want to ask."

Mom kept the knitting needles in her hands, but she lowered them to her lap. Joey-Mick stopped *thunk*ing the ball into his glove. Already they seemed to sense that what she had to say was important.

"This"—she pointed to the neat stack of bills—"is twenty dollars. And this—" She picked up the sock, turned it upside-down, and poured out the dimes. They made a silvery sound as they exited the sock. "This is five dollars in dimes. Twenty-five dollars altogether."

She looked right at Dad. Her next words came out in a steady stream, but not too fast—she wanted to be sure he heard every word. "I want to go to Ebbets Field to see a game, August fourteenth, Dodgers against the Giants, and I want to take the whole family plus some other people. Grandstand tickets are a dollar seventy each and I have enough here for the tickets *and* for bus fare for everybody, and I especially want to take Jim, because he loves baseball and he loves the Giants and maybe seeing a game will help him get better."

Maggie heard Joey-Mick's breath quicken. She

couldn't tell what Mom was thinking; her face didn't change one bit. But what they thought didn't matter.

Only one person mattered.

Dad spread his hands out in front of him. "Maggie-o, it's not the money," he said. "It's never been the money that's the problem."

Maggie was ready for that. "I know. But I had to think of—of some way to show you how much I want this." She clasped her hands and leaned forward a little. "Dad. Most of that is my confirmation money. From *January*. I didn't spend hardly any of it *this whole time*. And I been saving my allowance since then too. I never bought a single Hershey bar or gum—or anything—and the only thing I spent money on was the ice cream soda I got Joey-Mick on his birthday."

Silence.

"I saved enough for Jim's sister and her family, too. If they want to come. *And* George, in case you want another fireman to be there. You know, to make it safer."

More silence, Dad's face as unreadable as Mom's.

"Dad, I didn't do this for my own self. I mean, I always wanted to go to a game, but I—I know what you think about it, and I'd never be asking if it weren't for Jim. He's the reason I want to go. Well, the main reason anyway."

Next to her Joey-Mick bounced a little, then burst out, "Dad, if you and George go, we'd all be safe!" His voice slipped and skidded on the last word.

Maggie's stomach felt like the inside of a baseball—

miles and miles of string wound up hard as a rock. But on hearing Joey-Mick, something loosened just a little, and she almost felt like hugging him. She had been right not to let him in on the plan. It was lots better; he was way more eager now than he would have been if he'd known about everything in advance.

Then Mom spoke. "Ought to be able for seats near an exit, if you buy them early enough," she said.

Maggie's mouth fell open. She stared at her mother—first in disbelief, then in speechless gratitude. But Mom was already knitting away again, as if the conversation were about any old ordinary thing.

Maggie was suddenly exhausted. There was nothing more to say. She looked down at her hands without seeing them and waited.

The tiny clicking sound of Mom's needles nibbled at the silence. Joey-Mick fidgeted but didn't say anything. He was probably thinking the same as Maggie: Dad would decide now one way or the other, and that would be that.

Dad stirred the dimes on the table with one finger. "Guess you're not little kids anymore," he said at last. "You're old enough, the both of you, to understand and—and listen and do something the second I say so. In an emergency."

Maggie stopped breathing.

Dad picked up a dime and examined it closely. He turned it over and stared at the other side too, as if he had never seen a dime before in his whole life. At last he raised his eyes and looked at Maggie.

"I'll have to call Carol and see what she thinks."

"Dad!" Joey-Mick shouted and jumped to his feet. He banged into the table and almost fell over. The dimes hopped and slid a little.

Unable to speak, Maggie took the biggest breath she had ever taken in her life.

"Now, you be getting that money off the table before you lose any of it," Mom said.

Maggie gathered the dimes back into the sock. She was surprised to find that her fingers were all trembly.

"Catch, Maggie-o."

Dad winked at her and tossed her the last dime. And even though her hands were shaky, she caught it just fine.

Eleven

THE PLAN, PART TWO

*T*he pennant race was still a mad scramble among four teams, with the Giants in first place. Maggie had Dad purchase the tickets for the game—*the* game—a week in advance. With the race so close, she was afraid that all the seats would sell out. And the timing suited Dad, too; he was able to choose seats in the lower deck along the third-base line, in the second-to-last row. Near an exit.

Seven tickets. Maggie and the family, that was four. And Treecie and Jim and Jim's sister, Carol, three more. George had been invited, but he would be on duty that day. Maggie had worried that her dad might change his mind when they found out George couldn't go, but nothing more had been said about it.

Carol had told Dad that she would leave her boys at home with her husband.

"It's gonna be Jim's first real outing," Dad said, "so she figures it'd be better if she could concentrate on helping him. Without the boys there."

"Did he say anything?" Maggie asked. "I mean, did Carol say he said anything, when she told him about the game?"

"I don't know," Dad said. "Well, not that she mentioned to me."

Maybe Jim *had* said something, or at least responded in some way. Or maybe he hadn't, and he didn't really care, and it was Carol making him go. But Maggie couldn't quite believe that. Jim loved baseball and especially the Giants. Of course he would want to go to a game.

At any rate, everyone else was excited. Joey-Mick kept talking about catching a foul ball. Treecie was going to bring her camera and take pictures. "Action shots," she said. "They might not come out very good, but it'll be good practice."

Dad decided on the seating arrangement. "I want kids sitting next to adults," he said. "I'll take the aisle seat. Rose, I want you at the other end. Then Joey-Mick, then Carol and Jim. Maggie-o, you'll sit next to Jim, and Treecie will sit next to me. Everybody got that?"

Perfect. Treecie on one side of her, Jim on the other, without even asking. They would all be together. In Ebbets Field. *At a Dodgers game!*

The morning of the game, five of them—the family plus Treecie—went on ahead to Ebbets Field. Carol and Jim had to drive in from New Jersey, so it was decided that they would park near the firehouse to avoid the traffic downtown. They would pick up their tickets, which would be left at the firehouse. Then they would take the bus and meet the rest of the group at the ballpark.

Maggie had been disappointed when she learned that Jim and Carol would be arriving at the game separately. But it turned out to be a good thing, because when she first got to the ballpark, there was so much to see—she couldn't possibly have paid attention to Jim at the same time.

Once off the bus, they joined the streams of fans walking to the park's entrance. Everyone was in a good mood, it seemed. The talk was all about baseball; Maggie felt like even the air she was breathing was full of baseball somehow.

So many people! Maggie thought in pairs: Men / women; young / old; rich / poor; black / white . . . She spotted a priest in his collar and, a few moments later, two nuns in their habits. An enormously fat man, a bunch of really skinny boys. Ladies in suits and hats and gloves; men in worn caps and stained dungarees. It seemed as if the whole world loved baseball.

Treecie jabbered away at her side; Maggie listened without really hearing. She couldn't speak herself; she just kept looking and looking. . . .

"Over here," Dad called. He and Joey-Mick led the way, and as they walked side by side in front of her, Maggie noticed how tall her brother had grown lately. *He'll be taller than Dad any day now.*

Maggie had expected that Ebbets Field would be special, like magic almost, but she still wasn't prepared for what she saw as they walked into the entrance rotunda.

Where to look first—at the dazzling height of the ceiling that rose several stories above her head? At the enormous chandelier that had baseball bats for arms and big glass globes shaped like baseballs? At the marble floor, so smooth underfoot, a Dodgers baseball logo in the middle, with even the *stitches* made out of tiles—who had thought of *that?* Maggie had never seen a building as wonderful as the rotunda. Only the library came close.

People were swirling every which way; there didn't seem to be any kind of order to where they were going. But Dad had it all worked out. He led them through the rotunda toward one of the entrances to the stands. Maggie hardly noticed that they had to wait their turn for the crowd of fans to funnel their way through the entrance; she was too busy trying to make sure she saw absolutely everything there was to see.

Soon they were in what seemed like a maze—ramps and corridors and stairs that kept leading upward. It was darker here, all steel beams and dull brick and concrete floors. After the majesty of the rotunda, Maggie felt a little pinch of disappointment, but she did her best to ignore it.

"It's like a mystery!" she shouted to Treecie.

"What?" Treecie shouted back.

"Never mind." Maggie's thoughts didn't want to come out in words.

Elbows and shoulders bumped her. Someone stepped on her heel; her shoe almost came off, but she managed to stamp her foot and get it back on. Thank goodness—it would have been scary to have to bend down in that crowd.

Dad strode up a set of concrete steps, then turned aside to let the rest of them pass. He was grinning, looking right at Maggie. She grinned back, then glanced beyond him.

One more step, and—

After the darkness of the corridors, the sunshine was suddenly, blindingly bright. After the cramped and closed-in ramp, a huge free space opened out before her.

GREEN!

Maggie gasped. Her heart began pounding, her knees trembling. For a brief breathless moment she thought she might faint.

The perfect green diamond of the infield, outlined by white lines and base paths so precise they looked like a painting. . . . The great expanse of the outfield, trimmed by the warning track and held in by the wall, the grass fresh, smooth, greener-than-emerald, stretching on and on. . . . And the sky was an enormous bowl of purest blue overhead. Maggie had never seen so much grass and air and space in one place!

Maggie stared at the field every second as Dad herded them into their seats. She could have looked at that vast open greenness for years and years and never gotten tired of it.

"Look!" Joey-Mick leaped to his feet. "It's Jackie! *Look, over there!"* He pointed at a door in one corner of the outfield from which the players were beginning to emerge.

It was Jackie, all right. And Pee Wee, and Gil, and Campy, and the Duke. . . . Maggie had seen their pictures in the paper, and she thought they looked exactly like she had imagined they would look, only more so. Not as . . . *fancy*, but in a good way. Like ordinary guys who happened to be really good at baseball.

Then part of the crowd began booing, but it sounded almost friendly. Maggie turned her head to see the Giants coming onto the field. Mixed in with the good-natured boos were some cheers from the Giants' fans scattered throughout the stands.

Maggie watched as more Giants came out, their gray visiting-team uniforms trimmed with black.

There.

Loping across the grass to catch a ball that had been tossed to him by a teammate.

Number 24. Thanks to the photo Jim had given her, she'd have known him anywhere.

Willie Mays.

For the first time since they had arrived at the park, Maggie wondered where Jim and Carol were. She wanted to turn to Jim's empty seat and shout, "Jim— d'you see him? It's Willie!"

She looked behind her at the steps to see if they were coming. Why were they so late? The game would be starting soon—they might miss the first pitch. . . .

But in a moment Maggie was distracted again— Russ Meyer, the Dodgers' pitcher, was warming up along the foul line; the umpires came out; the teams began making their way toward their dugouts.

Maggie felt almost like she was dreaming. One after another, the things she had heard so many times before on the radio were happening *right in front of her*, only now with far more than just sounds and words. The green of the field, the confusion of colors in the stands, the smell of popcorn and hot dogs, the feel of the breeze on her skin. The announcer . . . the organ . . . standing for the national anthem . . . clapping and cheering when the Dodgers took the field. . . .

Somewhere along the way, Maggie had been given a scorecard for the game. She didn't remember anyone handing it to her; it must have been during those first few glorious moments of seeing the field. She couldn't decide whether to score the game in the scorecard, where the players were already listed in the batting order, or use her notebook, which of course she had brought with her. She finally chose the notebook. *I don't want a game missing from it. Especially not this one.* And she would keep the scorecard as a souvenir. Maybe she could copy her notations into it later.

Russ Meyer threw the first pitch of the game, and Maggie recorded it with a shiver of pure delight.

It wasn't until Willie came to bat later in the inning that she thought to look for Jim again. She'd had too much to worry about: The Giants had wasted no time, getting three hits in a row and scoring two runs with their first four batters. But when Willie came to the plate, Maggie took her eyes off him long enough to glance toward the steps.

Dad was standing at the corner where the steps met the aisle. He was watching the game, but after each pitch, he would turn and look down the steps. Maggie looked at him until their eyes met, then gave him a little wave of thanks.

Dad had it covered. He wouldn't miss them when they came.

Willie grounded out that first time at bat. The next batter got a hit, another run scored, and the Dodgers brought in Clem Labine to replace Russ Meyer. Maggie felt sorry for Meyer, leaving the game so early, but she was glad for Mom, who would now get to see her favorite pitcher.

The second inning was uneventful, for which Maggie was grateful. She had been almost over-whelmed by all the sights and sounds of the ballpark; it was much harder to concentrate on scoring the game here than at home listening to the radio. She hadn't realized before how helpful it was to have the radio announcer's commentary to focus her attention on each pitch. Twice she had to ask Joey-Mick if the strike call had been for swinging or looking.

In the third inning, the Giants' Alvin Dark singled for the second time. Then Labine threw a wild pitch, which sent Dark to second.

With two out, it was Willie's turn at bat again. Maggie tapped her pencil anxiously against her score-book. She wanted Willie to do well, but the Dodgers were already down by three runs.

Joey-Mick yelled, "C'mon, Clem! Strike him out!"

Maggie refused to look at her brother. She knew why he had yelled that—to jinx any wish she might have had for Willie to get a hit.

A bunt, she decided. *A bunt for a base hit. That way Willie gets a hit but Dark won't be able to score.*

Instead, Willie hit a single to center field and drove in a run. The Giants were now ahead, 4–0.

Two innings later Willie doubled over left fielder Sandy Amoros's head to drive Dark in *again.* That was two runs batted in for him.

Five to nothing, Giants. Joey-Mick pounded at the pocket of his glove in frustration. Maggie knew that if he could have, he'd have been pounding her arm instead. Her fault, for picking Willie as her favorite player . . .

Meanwhile, the Dodgers were helpless against Giants pitcher Ruben Gomez. They were coming to bat in the bottom of the sixth inning.

And still no Jim.

By now an unhappy restlessness had spread through the crowd. Ebbets Field was packed, as Maggie had guessed it would be, with the pennant race so close. The Dodgers' followers seemed equally divided between those who kept shouting encouragement at the players and those who had begun expressing their disappointment with boos and catcalls.

Maggie stared down at her score sheet. It seemed like *years* since the excitement of seeing the rotunda and the field; she could hardly believe it was the same day.

The Dodgers were losing badly. And Jim hadn't shown up.

Before the game, Maggie had been torn: Should

she hope—silently, of course—that the Giants would win, so Jim would be happy? She had been thinking about it for weeks, really, ever since it looked as though her plan might work.

August, and the end of the season so close. . . . Every game counted. How could she hope for the Giants to win when one game might mean the title? Finally, she had done her best to stop thinking about it at all. What happened would happen, she had told herself. And kept telling herself.

Now she stuck out her chin and sat up straighter.

Enough was enough. Jim hadn't come; he had ruined her perfect plan.

Maggie glared at the field.

"C'mon, you Bums!" she yelled as loud as she could.

Twelve

AFTER THE GAME

$\mathcal{I}$f Dad had been a mother hen on the way to the game, he was a mother grizzly bear on the way home. Whereas folks had arrived at the park over a period of a few hours, everyone left at the same time, close to thirty thousand people pouring into the streets at once. Which was, as Joey-Mick pointed out, a hundred twenty thousand arms and legs, every one of them moving.

Dad spoke to the little group before they left their seats. *"Stay together,"* he growled. "And stay cool, everybody."

Outside the park, as they waited their turn to board the bus, they were surrounded once again by talk about baseball. It was gleeful talk—no, better than that. Everyone was *ecstatic.*

Brooklyn had come all the way back from five runs down and won the game, 6–5. In the most thrilling way: a grand-slam home run by Carl Furillo in the sixth inning, and then a single by Roy Campanella in the seventh inning that brought home two more runs.

"I just *knew* he was gonna do it," Treecie kept saying, her voice a little hoarse from all the shrieking she had done when Campy got his hit. "I think I got the shot, too—I clicked right when he hit the ball, I'm pretty sure."

Gil Hodges and Jackie Robinson had scored on Furillo's home run, so both Mom and Joey-Mick were delighted with their favorite players. Willie Mays had gotten two hits and batted in two runs. Really, it couldn't have been more perfect: Willie had had a great game, but the Dodgers had won. They were now only a game and a half behind the Giants in the pennant race.

And Maggie had never in her life felt so unhappy.

The two seats for Jim and Carol had stayed empty until the eighth inning, when Mom and Joey-Mick finally moved over to close the gap. Throughout the last few innings, the shadow of Jim's absence grew darker and heavier in Maggie's mind, dimming the shine of the glorious relief pitching by Dodger Jim Hughes.

Dad had tapped her shoulder in the seventh inning. "Something musta come up," he said. "They prob'ly called the house, but we'd already left."

Maggie had nodded glumly. She knew he was trying to make her feel better, but he couldn't. No one could.

During the game, the lump of disappointment in her throat had gotten big enough to threaten tears a few times. Now, as she stood in line for the bus, the lump was gone, replaced by an ache in her jaw from clenching it. She flipped her notebook open and looked one more time at her scoring notations for the Dodgers' runs, especially the exclamation points for Furillo's grand slam and Campy's game-winning single.

Serves Jim right that we won, she thought. *We're gonna catch them now. We'll win the pennant, the World Series too, and that'll show him. . . .*

Maggie slapped the notebook closed in grim triumph. But as she followed Mom onto the bus, she wondered: *Show him what?*

Once they were off the bus in their own neighborhood, they walked in a loose group down the street, everyone except Maggie still chatting about the game. As they neared the firehouse, Maggie saw the guys seated in their folding chairs out front. Except for George, who was standing. But there were still four people sitting there—who was in the fourth chair?

It was a woman.

Carol, Maggie thought, and almost choked on her next breath. *Where's Jim?*

"Hey there!" Dad had seen her, and hollered a greeting from half a block away.

The woman stood and walked toward them. Dad limped a little faster, his hand stuck out in front of him.

"Glad to meet you," he said as he reached her and shook her hand. "This is my wife, Rose." Mom shook hands, too.

Carol was tall and had brown hair and brown eyes,

like Jim. She was wearing a black skirt and a white top. The Giants' team colors.

"I'm so sorry," she was saying. Then she looked right at Maggie. "You must be Maggie." A smile.

Maggie nodded and tried to smile back.

"I'm sorry," Carol said again. "We got here in plenty of time, but then—" She stopped and glanced at Dad.

Maggie saw their eyes meet. Then Dad turned to Mom. "How about some lemonade at the house?" he said. "Son, you go on and help your mother. Treecie, you too. Maggie will be right along."

Mom and Joey-Mick and Treecie walked on toward the house. That left Maggie standing at one side of the bay with Dad and Carol and George.

Whatever was going to be said next, Maggie would hear it too.

"We left our house fine," Carol said. "But when we got here, he wouldn't get out of the car. I tried talking to him for a while, and George tried, too. I ended up—" Her voice dropped. "I yelled at him." Then she looked away from them.

Maggie saw what Carol was looking at: a blue sedan parked farther down the street, with someone in the passenger seat.

Jim. He's sitting right there.

It was far enough away that she couldn't see him clearly, but she could tell that his head was down.

"He wasn't going nowhere," George said quietly.

"I told him, if he wasn't going to the game, we were

going to stay right here until you all got back so I could explain," Carol went on.

"That was good of you," Dad said. "Sorry you had to wait so long. We're just glad you're safe. I was hopin' it wasn't car trouble or an accident or something."

Carol stared at the ground. "I've never yelled at him before," she whispered. "But I was so mad—we came all this way, and I know how hard Maggie worked for this, and I thought that just this once he could manage to get himself. . . ." She couldn't go on, and Maggie saw her blink several times.

Maggie's jaw unclenched. All the anger and disappointment inside her seemed to dissolve into a huge puddle of tiredness and sadness. Her plan had not only failed, it had made things worse. It had made Carol yell at Jim, and now everything was terrible.

She felt a touch on her arm. "Maggie, just so you know," Carol said. "I thought it was a terrific idea, to get him to a game. I wish things could have worked out better—maybe it's still too soon. We can try again sometime, okay? And the tickets will be my treat."

Maggie didn't look up, but she nodded politely.

"Well." Dad put his arm around Maggie's shoulders. "How about some lemonade before you go back, Carol? You're welcome to stay for dinner, too."

"Thanks," Carol said, "but we should get on the road. We have a long drive ahead of us."

Dad and George began discussing the best route out of Brooklyn. Maggie looked at the blue sedan again.

She had been thinking about it for days, what she

would say to Jim when she first saw him. She had rehearsed dozens of conversations in her head until finally she had it all planned out. Maggie just *had* to talk to him now.

She started walking down the street toward the car.

"Maggie . . ."

Dad was calling, but she didn't turn back.

The car's windows were rolled down. She stopped by the front passenger door and took a breath to brace herself.

Jim was staring at the dashboard.

Maggie had imagined that he might look really, really sad. But that wasn't it, not at all. In some ways he looked the same. The flattop haircut, and even seated hunched over inside the car, he still looked tall.

But he looked different, too.

The shadows under his eyes were so dark, they looked like bruises. And his face . . .

Maggie had never seen anyone who looked the way Jim did now. His face was empty, his eyes blank. *When I look at someone's face, what I'm really seeing is them. I'm looking right at him—but he's not there.*

Maggie felt shaky all over. She put one arm over her stomach and pressed hard, to steady herself. She cleared her throat.

"Hi, Jim," she said, her voice small.

He didn't move, didn't look at her. She didn't even know if he had heard her.

Maggie fumbled with her notebook, which gave her a moment to swallow. "I had an idea. . . ." She turned the pages until she reached the spread with that day's game. Then she held it up so he would be able to see it.

If only he would look at it. Or at her.

She almost gave up then. *This isn't working. It's stupid. I'm stupid for thinking I could help him get better when nobody else could, not the doctors, not his family. . . .*

But she was standing there with the scorebook open and her plan for what she would say in her head, so she kept going.

"Gil Hodges walked here, in the sixth," she said, pointing to the right spot on the page. "And Sandy Amoros did, too. And then there was an error, and after that Carl Furillo hit a home run. So those two walks, they were just as good as hits, right?"

She didn't look up from the score sheet because she didn't want to see what she could feel: that he still hadn't moved, not one single inch.

"They keep track of a guy's batting average, but if he walks, it doesn't count," she said. "And I think there should be some way . . . I mean, if he's patient at the plate, and has a good eye, and gets a lotta walks"—she was speaking faster now—"that should count for something, don't you think? Because, like I just said, a walk can be as good as a hit sometimes."

Her last words had come out in a high-pitched rush, and the silence that followed was so heavy, she could hardly breathe. She stood trembling for a moment longer, then closed the scorebook slowly.

Nothing.

She held the book against her chest, as if it could shield her from that dreadful silence.

Just then she felt a nudge against her leg. Charky looked up at her and then at Jim, and whined softly.

Maggie could have thrown her arms around the dog, she was so relieved not to be alone anymore. Instead, she petted his head, then curled her fingers into the warmth and softness of the fur around his neck. And now here was Dad coming along the sidewalk.

"Hey, Maggie-o," he said and patted her on the back. "Ready for some lemonade?" Then he leaned over a little and looked in the car window. "Hey, Jim. Good to see you again."

Maggie could hardly believe how normal he sounded. But still no response from Jim.

"Listen, I'm around if you ever wanna talk," Dad said. "Like we used to. Gimme a call when you feel like it."

He straightened up and held out his hand. "Come on, Maggie-o. Charky, let's get you back to the guys."

She took his hand. Charky gave one more soft little whine in Jim's direction, then followed Maggie and Dad back up the street.

Thirteen

THE NEW PLAN

That night as she lay in bed, Maggie tried to think of all the good things that had happened. The smooth arc of the ball against the sky when Furillo hit the grand slam. The four Dodgers crossing the plate one by one, each waiting to congratulate the others, with Giants catcher Wes Westrum standing off to the side like someone left out of a party. Treecie's shrieks when Campy had singled home the last two runs.

It was no use. No matter what she tried to think of, she ended up in the same place: standing at the car, with Jim staring straight ahead, that dreadful emptiness in his eyes. *I should have talked about something different. Not about the walks. Not something that reminded him of the game.*

There must have been a *reason* why her plan to take Jim to a game hadn't worked. Maggie didn't like thinking about it, but that didn't make it go away.

Of course she wanted Jim to get better, and she really had thought that going to a game would help.

But the truth was, *she had wanted to go to a game.* Helping Jim—that had given her a good excuse. She never would have asked Dad otherwise, knowing how he felt about crowds.

She squirmed, burying her face in her pillow. It was almost as if she had *used* Jim to get to a game herself. Was that why her plan hadn't worked?

It had to be enough just for Jim to get better. Maybe Maggie should even give something up in exchange. People made sacrifices when they wanted something badly, didn't they? Those saints she had studied in confirmation class—they were always giving up the ways of the world, and then miracles happened.

There were sacrifices in baseball too—sacrifice flies and sacrifice bunts, where a runner was on base and the batter made an out *on purpose* to help the runner advance to the next base. In fact, the sacrifice bunt was one of Maggie's favorite plays. The bunt had to be just right. *Four* fielders would be ready to charge the ball—the pitcher, the catcher, the first and third basemen—and the batter had to push it far enough so none of them could get it easily, but at the same time gently enough so it would roll slowly and give the runner on base more time to advance. All that trouble, and the batter knew he was giving up any chance for a hit himself.

Well, she *had* made sacrifices for her plan to go to the game. She had given up lots of things she liked to do, like buying egg creams and candy. It hadn't been easy, saving her money all those months.

But it seemed like that didn't count, because in the

end, she had gotten something out of it. She had been able to go to the game.

Now maybe there was only one way left for her to try to help Jim. To chase that awful look out of his eyes and get him to talk again.

That would be worth a really *big* sacrifice.

Maggie could go almost anywhere in the neighborhood on her own now, but the rule was that she always had to tell Mom where she was going.

"I need to go to church again tomorrow," Maggie said. "I want to say a novena for Jim to get better."

A novena. A special kind of praying. Nine days, nine candles, nine prayers. It was one of the things you did when you needed a saint's help. When you couldn't get what you needed on your own.

She saw the doubt in Mom's face.

"After I'm done, I'll come straight home," Maggie said. "It won't take long."

"It's not your being out and about I'm thinking of," Mom said. "It's just that . . . Maggie, things don't always turn out the way you hope, and I'd want you to be understanding that."

"But it worked for you, so I thought maybe—"

"Whatever are you talking about?"

"Treecie told me. A long time ago. Remember, when Gil Hodges was in that really bad slump, and he got benched and everything? Treecie's mom told her that you asked for prayers for him. At knitting circle."

"Oh. Treecie was telling you that, was she."

Another brief silence, then Mom sighed. "Sometimes prayers get answered, and sometimes they don't," she said. "It's a simple fact, it is."

Maggie had already figured that out. It seemed like praying *did* work, at least part of the time. Like her prayers for the Dodgers. They still hadn't won the World Series, but they had always been right in there with a chance.

What she couldn't work out was *why* some prayers worked and others didn't.

"But if you want something really bad, and—and it's not something selfish, it's for somebody else—doesn't God . . . I mean, wouldn't He—"

"No," Mom said. "That isn't how it works." Then she checked herself, shaking her head. "I shouldn't be saying that. I don't know how it works, so I wouldn't know how it doesn't work, either."

Maggie couldn't decide if Mom's words made things better or worse. On the one hand, it was disappointing that Mom wasn't being more helpful—that she didn't have a special secret about how to make prayers work. On the other hand, it made Maggie feel it was okay to be confused about it, because it seemed that grownups were confused too.

She sighed. "I have to do *something*," she said. "I mean, if there's a chance that this might help—even just a little chance—then I have to try. Don't you see?"

Mom drew in a breath and nodded. "Yes, I do," she said. She reached out and gave Maggie a quick hug that turned into a little shake. "So long as you see, too."

* * *

Maggie still had a lot of dimes left because she had bought only seven tickets to the game. On the Monday morning after the game, she put a dime in her pocket. So slim and light, yet she could feel it there all the way to the church.

The church stood back from the street a little, five wide, shallow concrete steps leading to the big wooden doors. She pulled open one of the heavy doors, stepped inside the dim quietness, and stood still, letting her eyes adjust. Then she walked to the bank of candles at one side of the nave.

Maggie hadn't told Mom quite everything about her plan for the novena. The prayers would actually be for two things. For Jim to get better, of course. But to prove how much she wanted it, Maggie had decided to make that big sacrifice and pray for something else as well.

For the Giants *to win the pennant and the World Series.*

Maggie put her dime through the slot in the wooden box, took a new candle, and lit it. She placed it carefully among the others that were burning.

She stared at the candles for a while. Their little flames were mostly steady, but a flicker or two revealed the drafts of air wafting through the nave.

Now she walked to the back row of pews and crossed herself. She entered the pew, knelt, closed her eyes.

It won't count unless I mean it. With all my heart, no cheating.

Maggie opened her eyes and stared at the wooden back of the pew in front of her.

Pray for the Giants to beat the Dodgers?

I can't do this. I can't do it and really mean it.

Another voice inside her head: *Yes, you can. All you have to do is think of Jim—how he looked.*

She reached into her pocket and took out her rosary. The beads were smooth and cool under her fingertips.

Holy Mary, Mother of God . . .

Maggie crossed herself again, got to her feet, and left the pew. She stopped for one more look at her candle. It would be there tomorrow, and the next day, and the next, and each day she would put another dime through the slot and add another candle, until she had done it nine times altogether.

It seemed like a special sign that a novena had nine candles. Just like the nine innings of a baseball game.

For the rest of the season, Maggie felt as though she was being torn in two. She *couldn't* wish for the Dodgers to win. That would be going against her novena, which might be a sin—she wasn't sure, but it certainly felt wrong.

Maybe it wouldn't matter. If Mary, Mother of God, and all of Heaven were working on the novena, surely whatever Maggie was thinking wouldn't make a bit of difference. . . .

But even as that thought formed in her head, Maggie knew it was utterly dishonest. After all, the whole idea of praying for the Giants to win meant giving up the possibility of the Dodgers' winning. It wasn't like wanting Willie to do well and wanting the Dodgers to win at the same time. It had to be one or the other, and now that she had begun making the novena, she had to stick to it.

But she also found that she couldn't *not* wish for the Dodgers to win. Cheering for the Bums had been part of her days for so long, it seemed as if it was now part of *her*. She was a Dodgers fan. It was as simple as that. There was no way she could listen to a game without wanting them to win.

There was only one solution.

Maggie stopped listening to the games.

It almost killed her. In fact, she was pretty sure it *would* have killed her if it hadn't been for the fact that she only had to make it through a couple of weeks before school started again. A new school, junior high, and instead of walking she would take a bus there. But her head was crammed with so many thoughts about baseball and Jim that there was hardly any space left to think about school.

Those two weeks were the longest of her whole life. She had to leave the house whenever a game started because Joey-Mick or Mom would be listening to it. Even when they weren't, the temptation to turn on the radio was too strong.

She would go to the firehouse and take Charky to the park. Charky was always happy to see her, and if he wondered why their outings were suddenly so much longer than usual, he never asked.

Maggie always had to hurry to get to the park because the radios up and down the block would be on full blast. At times she could hardly bear it, and she would take off running as fast as she could, away from the sound of the game, away from the possibility that she might listen for a pitch or two and get sucked into the game and start rooting for the Dodgers.

Of course, not listening to the games meant that she wasn't scoring them, either. She had put her scoring notebook away the very evening she made the first prayer of the novena. The last Dodgers' game she had scored was on August 15, the day after the one at Ebbets Field. As she closed her closet door, she tried to console herself with the knowledge that Brooklyn had won both of those games.

For eight more days Maggie went to the church and lit a candle for Jim. She thought it would get easier, but each time she had to have the same silent argument, thinking that she couldn't be sincere, knowing that she had to be.

On the last day of the novena she stayed at the church a little longer than usual, standing before the bank of candles and watching them burn.

It was up to Heaven now. Heaven, with maybe a little help from Willie Mays.

Even though she wasn't listening to the games, Maggie continued to read the newspaper; after all, she had to see how the Giants were doing. Each night she checked the league standings. The Dodgers had a hot streak in the middle of September, winning seven games in a row. With nine games left in the season, the race was still nerve-strainingly close.

After yet another game-long walk in the park,

Maggie returned to the firehouse with Charky a few steps ahead of her.

"Hey, Maggie-o!" George called. He was putting away his folding chair; as usual, he had been sitting out front listening to the game.

"Hi, George. Just bringing Charky back," she said. She unclipped the leash and went inside the bay door to hang it on its hook.

As she came out, George gave her a look. "Dodgers lost," he said.

"Oh."

"Oh? That's all you got to say? Maggie, what's goin' on?"

"Nothing. I mean, nothing really."

George shook his head. "Look. I seen you taking Charks out every day at game time. You haven't listened to a game with us in more'n a week. You don't wanna tell me, fine, but don't tell me it's nothin' when I know it's somethin'."

Maggie glanced down at the pavement for a long moment. Then she looked up at George. "I can't tell you," she whispered.

"Can't? Or won't?"

She looked down again. The silence between them seemed to grow until it felt heavy on her shoulders and she slumped under its weight.

George sighed. "Maggie-o, it's not just lately. The time's comin' when you won't be hangin' around here as much anymore. And that's fine, that's the way it oughta be, you growin' up and all that. Happened with your brother, too. But listen here—"

He reached out and put one finger under her chin so he could lift her head and look right at her face.

"This house isn't goin' anywhere, and neither am I. So whatever it is, now or anytime or—or whenever—you be sure and lemme know if there's anything I can do to help."

He pulled his hand away. "That's all," he said.

Maggie cleared her throat. "Okay," she said. When what she really meant was, *Thanks with all my heart forever and ever and ever,* and it must have shown on her face because George nodded.

"Okay," he said. Then he got out his battered lunch box and opened it. He unwrapped his sandwich and took a big bite.

"Roast beef," he said as he chewed, "and horse-radish."

He held it out toward her.

Maggie hesitated. She didn't feel like eating just now. . . .

"Go on," he said.

She leaned forward and took a bite, the way she always had. The tang of horseradish filled her mouth, so strong it was almost like a pain, but delicious at the same time.

"Attagirl," he said.

Following their hot streak, the Dodgers lost five straight games, which took them out of contention. When the season ended, they were in second place, five games behind the pennant winners.

The Giants.

The Giants were going to the World Series!

Maggie found to her surprise that she was looking forward to the Series. Now that Brooklyn was out of it, she had no qualms about cheering for the Giants against the American League's Cleveland Indians. Some Brooklyn fans, like George, hated the Giants so much that they were rooting for the Indians. But Maggie knew that even George admired Willie Mays.

She took out her scorebook again to get ready for the Series. Opening it to the back pages, she felt a resigned satisfaction as she wrote "GIANTS" on one page and "INDIANS" on the other. Not as good as writing "DODGERS," of course, but she had missed keeping score.

And, although she tried not to think of it too often, it looked as if the novena might be working. . . .

After running home from school, Maggie got to hear a lot of the first game of the Series. It was a long, slow game that went into extra innings, the score tied, 2–2, and the Giants finally tallied the winning run in the tenth on a three-run homer by Dusty Rhodes.

Better still, as far as Maggie was concerned, was the play Willie made in the eighth inning. With two Cleveland runners on base, the batter Vic Wertz hit a fly ball to deep center. A double off the wall, for sure— Maggie closed her eyes and listened to the crowd roaring over the voice of the announcer; she could see the ball soaring farther and farther. . . .

But Willie had started running the instant the ball hit the bat. And he didn't stop. He ran and ran and ran,

and at the last moment he looked over his shoulder—
it was impossible, he'd never in a million years get
there in time—but the ball plunked into his glove and
then, even more impossibly, he spun around so fast
and threw the ball in so hard that the Cleveland runner on second base could only make it to third after
tagging up, and Willie's cap flew off as he fell down
from the force of his throw.

8!!!

B2F

Willie had saved a run from scoring, maybe even
two—runs that could have won the game for Cleveland. The three exclamation points didn't seem like
enough. Maggie wished she had a pen with gold ink to
record that play.

A few days later, when Giants pitcher Johnny
Antonelli got the last out in the last inning of the
fourth game, Maggie exhaled in a huge whoosh.

The Giants had won the World Series! Not just
won it but *swept*—they won it in four straight games!

Before she could stop herself, Maggie turned her
head to look at the phone.

*Silly—it's not like he's going to call right this
minute. . . .*

But her fingers were tingling and her heartbeat
seemed to have sped up a little, because she knew that
Jim must be *thrilled.* Even if he didn't call today,
maybe he was already talking again, and pretty soon he

would phone, or come over, even, and the two of them would talk about Willie's incredible catch and lots of other things.

Whenever the phone rang, Maggie jerked her head up and held her breath. But it was never Jim.

She could have called him herself. Gotten Carol's number from Dad, asked Mom for permission to make a long-distance call.

But what if Carol asked Jim to come to the phone and he wouldn't, and she ended up yelling at him again? That would be awful. No, it would be better to wait for him to call her.

The rest of the day went by, and then the rest of the week, with no call. Not even when the papers announced that Willie had been voted Most Valuable Player in the National League.

Jim's team winning the World Series—not just winning but sweeping all four games. His favorite player winning the biggest award . . .

And he *still* didn't call.

The best baseball news in the world hadn't been enough to help him.

Maggie took the scorebook to her bedroom. She had left it out on the shelf in the living room so it would be handy when Jim called to talk about the Series.

He wasn't going to call.

She opened the closet door. With her foot, she pushed aside last summer's sneakers so she could see the other scorebooks in the back corner.

All those books. All those pages. Hours and hours

and *hours* of listening to the games and writing everything down . . . and the Dodgers had never won the World Series, and Jim hadn't called.

Maggie turned and stomped toward her bed. She yanked the photo of Jim and Jay off the wall. A small corner of it tore and stuck to the wall; she pulled that piece off too. She jammed the photo between the pages of the latest scorebook and threw it onto the pile on the closet floor. Then she tossed her old sneakers on top and pulled some clothes off their hangers to bury the scorebooks good and deep.

She slammed the closet door shut and kicked it hard. She stood there panting a little and staring at the scuff mark her shoe had made.

I'm never keeping score again. Not ever.

For a brief moment, she felt almost frightened by the thought. But her eyes were dry. She pressed her lips together and stalked out of the room.

Fourteen

THE RAILWAY BRIDGE

$\mathcal{I}$t was the middle of November. Maggie stopped in at the corner store after school to say hello to Mr. Aldo and buy a Hershey bar. When she got home, she saw Dad sitting at the dining table.

"Hi!" Maggie said, pleased but puzzled. He never came home in the middle of the day.

"Hey, Maggie-o," Dad said. "You busy?"

"No, I was going to do some homework, but I can do it later."

"Good." He stood up. "Let's you and me go for a walk."

In that instant, Maggie knew what they were going to talk about. Not the exact words, of course, and she didn't know how she knew, but she did.

She waited while he got his coat; she hadn't taken hers off yet.

"Park?" she asked when they were outside.

"Sure," Dad said.

"Then can we take Charky with us?"

They stopped by the firehouse and said hello to the guys. When she got out the leash, Charky jumped around as if he had never been taken for a walk before in his whole life.

A short distance into the park, they found an empty bench. Maggie let Charky off the leash so he could go exploring. She wound the leash into a neat coil, waiting.

"Jim was here today," Dad said.

I knew it was gonna be about Jim. . . .

"Carol called this morning. She said that Jim had written her a note, that he wanted to talk to me. She was trying to act all calm and everything on the phone, but she was so excited that she got in the car with him and drove right over, and I got off work and came straight home."

Maggie couldn't decide what to ask first. "So what did he—I mean, how was—did he talk to you?"

Dad nodded. "Your mom and Carol had coffee. Me and Jim went for a walk."

Thoughts were crashing into each other inside Maggie's head. *It's like when George told me that Jim had written to Carol—well, he hadn't really, but that was what George told me—and I was jealous that he hadn't written to me. But this is worse! I'm the one who did everything! The game—and the novena—and the Giants—and saving my money for so long—*

For ages now there had been a picture in her head of how things would go. The Giants would win the World Series, and Jim would be so happy that he would start talking again, and she would be the first person he would want to talk to. And then other people—Treecie, probably, maybe Carol and Dad and Mom, too—would tell him how hard Maggie had worked and all the things she had done to help him get better, and he would be so grateful. And she would be sort of like a hero.

Stupid. *Stupid*. Maggie could feel her pulse thumping in her throat and she knew that her whole face had gone red. She turned away a little, hoping that Dad wouldn't notice.

"He didn't say anything until we got to the park," Dad said. "Then he started talking, but he could only sorta whisper. I guess 'cause he hasn't used his voice in so long."

Dad reached out and gave Maggie's hair a gentle tweak. "Maggie-o, when we got back home, before he left, I asked him—I said I wanted to tell you everything and I hoped he wouldn't mind. He didn't say yes—he was done talking by then—but he didn't say no, either. So I'm telling you, 'cause I think . . . I think you got a right to know."

Maggie's heartbeat slowed a little. She couldn't speak, but managed a nod.

"What happened to Jim, it was bad," Dad said. "I mean, bad things always happen in a war, that's just the way it is. But I guess there's some things you can't never expect."

Dad looked down for a moment. "You remember about the battle, right?" he said.

Maggie nodded.

"Well, it was a tough one. And it was even worse

because a report had come in from Recon that there were Commie spies around somewhere."

"Recon?" Maggie said.

"Reconnaissance," Dad said. "Those are the guys who go out ahead of everyone else and scout things and send back reports. Anyway, the reports said that the spies were dressed like civilians. To try to sorta blend in with the villagers.

"So during the battle Jim is going back and forth from camp to the front, bringing back soldiers who are hurt. Sometimes bodies too. And the fighting keeps going on, and he works through a day and a night without a break, and half the next day too. And on his last trips to the front, he's not bringing back soldiers anymore."

Dad stopped. Maggie didn't speak. She didn't blink or breathe, either.

"Civilians. People from the village, women, old men, kids." Dad turned toward her. "And while Jim was working on them, bringing them back, he talked to some of them, the ones who weren't hurt too bad, and it was clear that it was—that they had got hit by friendly fire."

He answered before she could ask. "Friendly fire—that's when you get hit by your own side."

Maggie gasped. "By your own side? How could that happen?"

He shook his head. "I guess things get pretty crazy in a battle like that. It might be a unit's supposed to be in one place, but somehow things get confused and they end up somewheres else, and then they get fired at because everyone thinks they're the Reds.

"What happened where Jim was . . . well, maybe nobody will ever really know. But these villagers, they'd been hurt by American weapons, he could tell that for sure. And some of them said it was on purpose. That it wasn't a mistake."

"No," Maggie said immediately. "It had to be a mistake." Why would soldiers shoot at people who were friendly to them—people whose village they were trying to protect?

"It was because of them spies," Dad said. "There was a bunch of villagers who took cover under a railroad bridge. A whole big crowd of them, all huddled together. The soldiers thought the spies were hiding in the crowd, but they couldn't tell who they were. So they just—"

Dad stopped and swallowed before he went on. "They shot at everybody. That's what Jim heard, but nobody knew for sure what really happened. And the worst of it was, there was this kid—"

Dread clogged Maggie's throat. "Oh, no," she choked out.

"Their tent boy." Dad was almost whispering now, the softest Maggie had ever heard him speak. "He was hurt real bad, and Jim and the medic worked on him out in the field, and they brought him back, but there wasn't nothing anyone could do. . . ."

Maggie felt as though the blood had stopped running through her body, like she might never be able to move again.

Dad cleared his throat. "Jim said when the fighting first got started, he sent the kid home. Told him to go back to the village, thought he would be safer there. So he blames himself, see—he thinks that if he hadn't sent the boy home, then he wouldn't have ended up under the bridge, and maybe . . ."

The words trailed off. It was quiet for a long time.

Maggie didn't know if he was finished talking, but she couldn't listen anymore. She stood up slowly. Her legs and arms felt like they each weighed a thousand pounds.

Dad took the leash from her and whistled for Charky. They took him to the firehouse and left him. Dad went in to hang up the leash while Maggie waited well away from the bay doors so she wouldn't have to talk to the guys.

She didn't say a word during the entire walk home.

But at the front door, she stopped and put her hand on her father's arm.

"His name was Jay," she whispered.

Maggie sat on her bed, holding the letter Jay had written to her.

The handwriting a little crooked and unsure, like a first grader's. And the whole thing was only eight words long.

But it was enough to make her feel as if she had known him. It was a piece of paper that Jay himself had touched, words that he had written with his own hand and sent especially to her.

She thought about him huddled under that railroad bridge, where everyone would have been scared, even the grownups, and then the soldiers showing up, and Jay must have thought they'd be safe now, the soldiers would protect them. . . . And then the gunfire starting, and everything going crazy, people screaming. . . . Jay terrified, until the moment he got shot himself—

She clutched the letter tightly. *He passed out right away—he never felt a thing.* That had to be how it happened. Anything else was too awful to imagine.

She thought about Jim too—what it had been like for him. To get to the scene and see all those people hurt—ordinary people, not armed, not soldiers—and start working on them and trying to save them even though he was already beyond exhaustion . . . and then to find Jay, unconscious and bleeding, and remember what had happened earlier—that it was he himself who had sent Jay home, sent him right into terrible danger. . . . Jim, his face stained with sweat and soot and blood, holding Jay's pale limp body . . .

She closed her eyes to shut out that last image. When she opened them again, she found herself staring at the shelf above her bureau. Her war notebook was there, and she thought of the maps she had drawn.

"The line," she whispered.

The line across Korea that showed how much territory each side had.

Dad hadn't said exactly when the battle happened. But it was sometime in the summer of 1952 for sure, because that was when Jim had stopped writing to her.

And she knew from her war notebook that the line hadn't changed since June 1951.

Maggie felt like she wanted to scream at somebody, beat them with her fists, kick them. But who? Whose fault was it? The government people? Why hadn't they just stopped the war, stopped the fighting, as soon as they saw that the line wasn't moving?

If we were getting more territory—if we were winning—if we were beating the Commies, then maybe—maybe there would be at least a chance to feel like it was worth it. Jay dying and Jim getting so sick—instead, it was for nothing.

Maggie made the sign of the cross against her thumb. Sometimes that helped make her feel a little calmer. This time, though, it made her think about how she hadn't begun praying for Jim until long after the battle, after he had been back in the U.S. for a good while.

At least I did pray for him. But I didn't pray for Jay at all.

Never. Not once.

Did it matter? Would it have made a difference? If she had prayed for him, would that have stopped the spies, the soldiers, the shooting?

She crossed her arms over her stomach, hugging herself hard.

No. Only little kids think like that. It wouldn't have made any difference. Just like scoring the games doesn't help the Dodgers.

Nothing I do changes anything.

Maggie wept.

*　　*　　*

The next day she learned that Dad had called Carol, only to find out that Jim had gone back to not talking.

The phone rang. It was Treecie.

"Can I come over?" she said. "I wanna talk about our birthdays."

Last year Maggie and Treecie had celebrated their birthdays together. They were getting too old for the little-kid kind of party; instead, their mothers had taken them downtown for lunch and shopping. Treecie probably wanted to do the same kind of thing again, only different.

"I guess so," Maggie said.

"What's wrong?" Treecie said immediately. "Never mind. I'm coming over, you can tell me when I get there."

Within a few minutes, Maggie heard Treecie's knock at the front door. Treecie came in and greeted Maggie's mom cheerily, filling up the place with her presence. Maggie had to smile a little. Treecie was like Dad that way; you always knew when either of them was around.

She came up to Maggie's room and sat on the bed next to her.

"Oh Maggie, I'm so sorry," Treecie said after Maggie told her about Jim and Jay-Hey. "That's awful, just awful."

Maggie blinked several times, hard. There wasn't any way to stop tears from filling your eyes once they had decided to do it. You could blink them away, but only after they were already there.

She swallowed before she spoke. "Treece, I feel so bad," she said. "I really, really wanted to help, but nothing I did—"

"That's not true," Treecie said. "You wrote to Jim all the time and you could tell how much he liked getting your letters 'cause he wrote back every time up until—well, as long as he could. And you know how much Jay liked those cards—he even learned to write English so he could thank you for them!"

"I know. But it didn't make any difference in the end."

Treecie thought for a moment, then looked Maggie right in the eye. "How do you know?"

"How do I know what?"

"How do you know it didn't make a difference?"

A little nettled now, Maggie sat up straighter. "What I mean is, this terrible thing happened, and there wasn't any way for me to stop it, and I can't even help Jim feel better about it, and nothing you say is gonna change that."

"And what *I* mean is, you don't know what's going to happen next," Treecie said, nettled right back at her. "Jim might still get better—I mean, he probably *will* get better, he talked to your dad, didn't he? I bet it was because he saw your dad after the game, and that was all your idea, to get everyone together for a game. So it isn't over yet, and you shouldn't talk like it is."

Maggie shook her head and stared down at the bedspread. "It's over for Jay," she whispered.

That shut Treecie up. Neither of them said anything for a while.

"Well," Treecie said at last, and her voice was quieter, "what are you gonna do now?"

Maggie looked at her. "I'll be fine, I just have to give it some time," she said—in a sarcastic pretend-grownup voice.

"Why do they always say that?" Treecie said, energetic again. "You don't care how you're going to feel *later*, you care about how you feel *now*, and they act like that doesn't matter."

She reached out and gave Maggie several exaggerated pats on the head. "'You're young, you'll get over it.'"

Maggie wagged her finger. "'Run along and play now.'"

Treecie stood and put her hands on her hips. "'Never mind, leave that to the grownups.'"

Maggie again: "'Forget it—you'll understand when you're older.'"

Treecie flung herself back down on the bed and spoke in her regular voice. "We understand plenty. And just because we don't understand everything doesn't mean we should forget. You won't ever forget Jay, even if you do feel a little better someday."

Then she looked at the wall and frowned. "Hey, what happened to his picture?"

Maggie bit her lip. "I put it away. To—to keep it safe."

Treecie snapped her fingers. "Hey, I know what," she said. She jumped up. "I'll be right back."

It was close to an hour before Treecie returned. She handed Maggie a brown paper bag.

"It's not your birthday present," Treecie said. "That's why I didn't wrap it. It's just a . . . present-present."

Maggie reached into the bag and pulled out a picture frame.

"It'll keep Jay's picture from getting torn or anything," Treecie said. "Where is it?"

"It's around here somewhere," Maggie mumbled. "I'll find it later."

Treecie started to say something, then stopped and studied Maggie's face. "Okay," she said.

Maggie opened her bureau drawer to put the frame away. "Thanks, Treece," she said. "It's perfect. Really."

She didn't say what she was thinking: that Treecie must have spent some of her precious camera money on this gift. Maggie found herself blinking hard again as she stroked the smooth wood of the frame for a moment before she closed the drawer.

Fifteen

PROOF

*M*aggie had just reached home after school when she heard loud voices down the street. It was Joey-Mick and his friend Davey.

"You're nuts!" Davey was yelling. "It was one-and-oh, not oh-and-one."

"Just you wait," Joey-Mick yelled back. "I'm tellin' ya—" He caught sight of her. "There she is—hey, Mags, wait up!"

Both boys ran the rest of the way, Joey-Mick's long arms and legs pumping, all elbows and knees. He beat Davey to the stoop by three steps.

"Maggie—remember the Thomson home run—" he panted.

Davey broke in. "I say the first pitch was a ball—"

"—and I say it was a strike. Branca had him oh-and-one—"

Maggie looked at Joey-Mick and then at Davey. "It was . . ." she paused dramatically. Neither of the boys moved, but she felt like they were both sort of leaning toward her.

"It was a strike," she declared. "And I can prove it, too!"

"I'll get it, I'm faster," Joey-Mick said, already in the house.

"In my closet!" Maggie yelled. "At the bottom!"

A short silence. Then Davey shook his head. "What'd you do, save an old newspaper or somethin'?"

Before she could answer, Joey-Mick burst out onto the stoop and waved the scorebook at Davey.

Maggie held out her hand. "I'll find it," she said.

"No, lemme do it." Joey-Mick began paging through the book. "Look—here it is, see that little backwards S? That's the pitch count, and backwards means strike looking. If it was a swing, she woulda made a regular S. Oh-and-one, that's what the count was, right there in black-and-white!"

Davey took the book and studied it for a moment.

"See?" Joey-Mick said again. "You owe me an egg cream!"

"Yeah, yeah," Davey muttered ungraciously. A pause. "How come you don't got the home run written down?"

It was true. Maggie remembered how she hadn't been able to fill in the square that day. "Didn't feel like writing it in," she said. "Stupid Thomson."

"Stupid Thomson," Davey echoed, shaking his head in disgust. He turned a few more pages. "Hey, look at this one, 13–1, over the Reds." He chortled. "Look at all those runs."

Then he looked up at Maggie and raised his eyebrows. "Pretty neat, Maggie-o."

"Thanks," she said. She could feel her cheeks getting pink.

"I gotta go," Davey said. "See you after supper, maybe."

Joey-Mick didn't even say goodbye; he was busy studying the scorebook. After a few moments he glanced up.

"Know what?" he said, waving the book at her. "This book makes you probably the biggest Bums' fan in the neighborhood. And around here that's sayin' somethin'."

For the first time in weeks, Maggie felt a little warmth inside her chest.

"It's like a—a country or somethin'," Joey-Mick went on. "Baseball, I mean. A place where everybody's crazy about the same thing. But you can't play 'cause you're a girl, so you found another way to—to live there, and talk baseball and everything. I mean, you know more about baseball than most of the guys I know!"

Maggie's eyes widened. That was a pretty long speech for Joey-Mick, and his voice hadn't cracked the whole time, not once. If Treecie had been there, she would have said what's the big deal, of course girls could learn about baseball same as boys. But Maggie knew that he meant it as a compliment. She tried to cover her surprise with a shrug, and tilted her head in thanks.

Then she sighed. "I don't know," she said slowly. "I

was thinking that . . . that I'm done keeping score. I'm not gonna do it anymore."

There. She had said the words out loud, and it felt even worse than thinking about it.

"Why not?"

"Well . . ." She looked up at him and then away. "This is going to sound really stupid, but when I was keeping score, it felt—I felt sort of like I was helping. I mean, I know I wasn't *really* helping, but . . ." She stopped.

Joey-Mick nodded and grinned. "One time I wore the same shirt ten days in a row 'cause they were on a winning streak."

"I remember that!" Maggie exclaimed. "Mom was really mad that you wouldn't let her wash it."

Then she lowered her head. "But none of that stuff helps, not really," she said. "So I figure it's just a big waste of time."

Joey-Mick handed her back the scorebook. "With some things, you don't know for sure."

She frowned. Hadn't Treecie said almost the same thing? "Don't know what?"

"Whether it's a waste of time or not." He shrugged. "All that time I spent playing baseball? And it turns out I'm way better at basketball." He cocked his head a little. "I'm gonna be first-string this season. Varsity. At guard. Coach told me today."

Varsity? Joey-Mick was only a sophomore. In baseball last season, he hadn't even been a starter on the *freshman* team.

Maggie had been to some of his basketball games.

He was good, all right, but she didn't know much about basketball, so she hadn't realized *how* good.

"Really? Wow. Gosh, that's pretty neat, Joey- Mick."

"Yeah," he said. "So you could say all that baseball practice was a waste of time. But maybe it wasn't. Maybe it taught me stuff that'll help me in basketball, too. I don't mean skills, but you know—discipline, focus, stuff like that."

Then he grinned. "Know what they started callin' me? 'Not-So-Teeny Joe.' But that was too long, so they tried 'Not-So Joe,' but that didn't make any sense, and then one of the guys said I was a maniac on the court, so now they're callin' me 'Nutso Joe.'"

"Nutso Joe. . . . Maybe that'll get shortened again, and you'll be plain old Nuts."

Joey-Mick made a fist and pretend-jabbed it at her. "You call me Nuts, I'll call you a taxi," he said.

Dumbest joke ever, but they both laughed anyway.

Maggie took the scorebook back to her room. All the others were on her bed, higgledy-piggledy; Joey-Mick must have thrown them there when he was looking for the right one. She picked up the books and sat down with them on her lap.

Five of them. 1951. The '51 playoffs. 1952, '53, '54.

It was always wait till next year.

Maggie opened the book on top of the pile. 1951. She leafed through it slowly. Page after page of little squares filled with tiny numbers and letters . . . and every square Maggie looked at brought pictures to her mind, all vivid with the colors and sensations of having been at a game herself.

Jackie dancing on the base path.

Pee Wee going deep in the hole.

Willie in center field, running toward the wall as fast as he could.

She could almost hear Red Barber's voice on the radio. Maggie held her breath, as if those plays were happening at that very moment. Would Jackie steal second? Who would get to the ball first—Willie or the wall? The crowd roaring in the background . . . and once, her own voice had been part of that crowd noise.

Her breath eased out slowly as she continued to turn the pages. Every game, every inning, every play—really, every *pitch* she had recorded in the book had been a chance to hope for something good to happen.

She shook her head and almost smiled. Dodger fans probably had more practice at hoping than fans of any other team. *The same thing over and over again, but always different.*

Prayers were like that, too. Her bedtime prayers— saying almost the same thing each night, but feeling a little different sometimes, depending on what she was praying for. And the novena. . . . She recalled the quiet and stillness in the church, the glow of the candles both fierce and lovely, her mind full of thoughts about Jim, hoping for him to get better.

Maybe praying was another way to practice hope.

If that was true, then between the Dodgers and praying, she ought to be getting awfully good at hoping.

Maggie sighed. *What's the use of getting good at it? Hope doesn't do anything.*

Another voice spoke up inside her head. *But hope is what gets everything started. When you make plans, it's because you hope something good is going to happen. Hope always comes first.*

One by one, she picked up the scorebooks and turned their pages, pausing now and then to recall the plays and the games. As she flipped through the last notebook, something fluttered to the floor.

It was the photo of Jim and Jay. Maggie bit her lip, remembering how furious she had been when she hid the picture there. She picked it up and fingered the torn corner.

Then she rose from the bed, took the frame Treecie had given her out of the bureau drawer, and put the photo carefully into the space behind the glass. The missing corner hardly showed at all.

Maggie spent the next few minutes clearing off the top of the bureau, putting away bobby pins, books, a pencil stub, other odds and ends. She picked up the scorebooks one by one and stacked them in order of their years, 1951 on the bottom. She put the scorebooks on top of the bureau, and took her war notebook down from its place on the shelf and put that on the stack, too.

Finally, she placed the framed photo of Jim and Jay carefully on top.

As she left the room, she turned back for a moment and stood in the doorway.

It was just right. She would see them every time she came into the room.

December, three days before her thirteenth birthday. Maggie walked home from the bus stop after school, thinking about the celebration that had been planned. Her and Treecie's joint birthday. They would be going downtown with Mom and Mrs. Brady to see a matinee and then have tea at a fancy hotel. They would get all dressed up, too; Treecie had said she was even going to wear a hat.

Maggie had Treecie's present ready. Last week, there had been a sale at the library. Many of the books looked pretty old, but others were in perfectly good shape and Maggie couldn't understand why they were being sold. Some cost only a nickel.

Browsing through the piles on the tables, Maggie had come across a spiral-bound book with lots of photographs in it. It was called *Women at Work: A Tour Among Careers.* Several of the pictures had been taken by Margaret Bourke-White.

Maggie knew that name. Treecie's hero!

As well as the photos, the book had stories about women who had interesting jobs. Maggie especially liked the essay by a woman named Dorothy Canfield Fisher. Mrs. Fisher had gone to France during World War I. She had worked with soldiers there, mostly those who had been blinded, and had also set up a shelter for children injured in the war.

Most of the women in the book were authors or journalists. They had traveled all over the country and to different parts of the world, and had written about a whole bunch of different subjects.

Maggie had found out that the official scorer for the Dodgers was a position rotated among the journalists who covered the game. It wasn't actually a separate job all by itself. You had to be a journalist first. And here were all these women journalists. . . .

So maybe I could be a journalist when I grow up. Listening, and then writing things down—kind of like scoring.

She could already hear Treecie's response to that: "What a great idea! We could travel together! You'll write the stories, and I'll take the pictures—we'd be a great team!"

Maggie had wrapped the book nicely and made a card. She was looking forward to Treecie's reaction when she opened the gift.

"Mail for you," Mom called from the kitchen when Maggie arrived home.

Maggie always got birthday cards or letters from both Ireland and Canada; she liked knowing that people so far away were thinking about her.

Two envelopes. She sat down at the table and looked at the stamp on the first one. Canadian. She slid her finger under the flap and took out a pink card with red roses on it. *"Thinking of you on your special day,"* it read on the front in fancy gold letters, and inside, *"Many happy returns of the day."*

Written at the bottom:

Maggie dear, can't believe you're thirteen!
We miss you.

Love from Aunt Maria
and Uncle Scott

Maggie walked across the room and reached up to stand the card ajar on the shelf above the radio; Mom always put cards there so everyone could see them. Then she went back to the table and picked up the second envelope.

An ordinary envelope, not card-shaped.

U.S. stamp.

Her name and address on the front.

Maggie drew in a sharp breath.

That handwriting. She had seen it many times before—on score sheets and letters. . . .

Inside the envelope was a folded piece of notebook paper. As she pulled it out, she could see that there was hardly any writing on it.

When she unfolded the piece of paper, it was upside down. She turned it right-side up and read:

Dear Maggie-o,
You're right about the walks.
Your friend Jim

She read it again. And again. Then she touched the words on the page with her fingertips, gently, gingerly, as if they were a flock of tiny birds that might at any moment fly away.

*   *   *

The next day Maggie took all the money she had left—five dollars and forty cents—and went to Mr. Aldo's store. It wasn't a big place; still, there was enough variety in the display that it took her several minutes to decide.

Maggie gave her selection to Mr. Aldo. She counted out two dollar bills and thirty dimes as he put her purchase into a paper bag.

There was no snow yet, but it was cold enough that Maggie ran the last half-block home, holding the bag carefully so as not to bump it.

Back at the house, she hung her coat on its peg in the hall and went up to her room. From the paper bag, she took out two fancy notebooks. They were more like journals, with real leather covers instead of plain cardboard.

One brown, one black.

Maggie put the black one back in the bag. She stroked the smooth leather of the brown one. She had wanted blue, but the choice had been black or brown. Maybe she could find a blue one next year.

She tried to guess where the exact middle of the book was and opened it carefully there. The spine creaked sweetly, as if the notebook was glad to be opened for the first time.

The pages were heavier than ordinary paper. Maggie riffled through them a few times; she liked the whispery sound of the riffling.

At last she turned to the first page. In the upper right-hand corner, using her best handwriting, she wrote:

Dodgers Scorebook
by Margaret Olivia Theresa Fortini
for the 1955 season

The black journal was for Jim. Black, the Giants' team color. Tomorrow she would mail it to Carol's house in New Jersey.

Opening Day was five long months away, but she would be ready, and maybe Jim would be, too.

Epilogue

In 1955, for the first and only time in their history, the Brooklyn Dodgers won the World Series, defeating the Yankees in seven games.

Acknowledgments

My thanks to:

Fred Vergara, Lisa DeVries Workman, Gerry Roth, and Dave Ruby, among many others, for helping nurture my childhood love of baseball. Freddy Berowski, Research Associate, A. Bartlett Giamatti Research Library at the National Baseball Hall of Fame & Museum in Cooperstown, N.Y., for assistance with key baseball facts and figures. The staff of the Brooklyn Public Library, for specific help with questions for this story, and for being there years ago, when I was a young mother in Brooklyn.

Ginger Knowlton, Marsha Hayles, Julie Damerell, and Michele Burns: my all-girl, all-star infield.

Dinah Stevenson, who sometimes has to drag me kicking and screaming toward a better story, but always does so with patience and wisdom and good humor. The staff at Clarion Books, especially Jim Armstrong (who has a picture of the 1955 Dodgers on his office wall), for blocking all those pitches in the dirt.

My husband and daughter, for putting up with my passion for baseball. My son, for sharing it. My dad, for taking me to games at Wrigley Field when I was a child, and my mom, for preparing the sushi picnics we ate during the games.

Any errors in the text are my responsibility.

Author's Note

Two seasons after the landmark World Series victory, Maggie would have mourned with all of Brooklyn when, at the end of the 1957 season, owner Walter O'Malley moved the Dodgers to the West Coast, where they became the Los Angeles Dodgers. The Giants went west as well, to San Francisco, taking Willie Mays with them. As much as it hurt New York fans at the time, the moves helped make baseball truly a national game.

After the two teams relocated to California, there was no National League team in New York for five years. In 1962, the New York Mets franchise was established, eventually with a new stadium in Queens. Maggie, like many Brooklyn fans, could never in a million years have become a Yankees fan, and I am pretty sure she eventually became a Mets fan. In 1972, she would have seen the return of Willie Mays to New York, where he finished out his career with two seasons as a Met.

I grew up in the Chicago area; as a child, I was a rabid Cubs fan. And like Maggie, I had a favorite player on another team—Roberto Clemente of the Pittsburgh Pirates. Whenever the Cubs and Pirates played each other, I would cheer for Clemente to do well but for the Cubs to win the game.

For the scenes depicting Maggie's disappointment at the Dodgers' many near-misses, I was able—alas!—

to draw on many memories from my years as a Cubs fan. Most of all, I recalled the 1969 season, when I was the same age as Maggie is when this book opens. In first place for most of the season, the Cubs lost a nine-game lead in an agonizing stretch during August and September. It was the Mets who overtook them and went on to win the pennant and the World Series.

Life sometimes throws you a curve ball, and these days, due to geographical and family happenstance, I am a devoted *Mets* fan. It took a while for those raw memories of 1969 to fade to sepia, but I have magnanimously forgiven the Mets and now follow their progress daily throughout the season. As of this writing, the Mets are constructing a new stadium (to be opened for the 2009 season). To my—and Maggie's—delight, it will have an entrance rotunda inspired by the one that graced Ebbets Field, and it will be named in honor of Jackie Robinson.

The score sheet on the endpapers for that fateful game between the Dodgers and the Giants in 1951 was produced exactly as Maggie would have done it: by listening to the audio broadcast of the actual game (ordered from baseballdirect.com) and marking down the plays as I heard them. Likewise, I listened to a recording of Game 1 of the 1954 World Series to score the play depicted on page 168—Willie Mays's catch of Vic Wertz's fly ball.

Scoring a baseball game is both neatly standardized and wildly personal. Some notations are recognized universally, but everyone I know who keeps score also has foibles and codes unique to themselves. On page 42, Jim "invents" the use of the exclamation point to denote an outstanding play. This was something I myself "invented" when I kept score as a child. At the time, I had never seen anyone else score a play this way, but years later I learned that it has become a notation standard.

Maggie develops a way to track the pitch count, as she explains to Jim on page 33. I got this idea from my son, who began rigorously recording the ball-and-strike count when he was only eight years old. There are now preprinted score sheets available that include an area to record the pitch count for each at-bat.

Maggie would be pleased that there is now indeed a statistic that includes walks as a measure of a player's ability to reach base. The on-base percentage (OBP), which includes a player's hits, walks, and getting hit by pitches, was first calculated in the 1950s (by Branch Rickey and Allan Roth) but was not adopted as an official statistic by Major League Baseball until 1984. When I was a child, a player's official stats did not include OBP (although the OBP of past players has since been calculated and is now available). Today it is considered one of the most important offensive numbers.

In 1980, the system of using journalists to serve as official scorers was abolished, and it is now, indeed, a separate job. Scorers are appointed by each team but are employees of Major League Baseball. If Maggie had become an official scorer, she would have been one of several women who have held that position throughout the years, beginning with Eliza Green Williams, official scorer for the Chicago White Sox from 1882 to 1891. However, Treecie would have been outraged at how few women there are even now in the top ranks of sports journalism and management.

Although I don't remember being taught to keep score, I do know who taught me: Fred Vergara, a lifelong family friend and baseball fan, whose own score sheets are works of art. I owe him a great debt for increasing my love of the game, and for giving me many hours of pleasure when I taught my son how to score.

Of the many sources I used to research this story, three were especially helpful. *Wait Till Next Year,* by Doris Kearns Goodwin, is a memoir about being a Brooklyn Dodgers fan in the 1950s. *We Were Innocents: An Infantryman in Korea,* by William Dannenmaier, includes letters written by the author during his years of service. *I Remember Korea: Veterans Tell Their Stories of the Korean War, 1950–53,* by Linda Granfield, contains first-hand accounts and archival photographs as well as an introduction by author Russell Freedman, who served in Korea. In addition to newspaper accounts, I relied on www.baseballlibrary.com, www.baseballalmanac.com, www.baseball-reference.com, and www.retrosheet.org for statistics and game details.

The tragedy of the civilians gunned down under the railway bridge described in Chapter 14 is loosely based on an incident that happened during the Korean

War. According to *The Bridge at No Gun Ri: A Hidden Nightmare from the Korean War,* by Charles J. Hanley, Sang-Hun Choe, and Martha Mendoza, South Korean civilians, including women and children, were killed by U.S. soldiers at a railway bridge near a village called No Gun Ri in July 1950. Hanley *et al.* won a Pulitzer Prize for Investigative Reporting in 2000.

My parents were teenagers in Korea during the war. From its inception until 1998, the tragedy in Korea was officially known as "the Korean conflict"; as Dad tells Maggie on page 123, Congress never declared war on North Korea. In 1998, President Bill Clinton signed an act of Congress that changed the designation to "the Korean War."

A cease-fire has been in existence in Korea since 1953. A cease-fire is defined as not an end to hostilities but a pause in the exchange of fire. Both South and North Korea and their allies have thousands of soldiers who patrol the border (known as the Demilitarized Zone, or DMZ) in a constant state of armed readiness. A peace treaty has never been signed.

Which means that as of this writing, the Korean War is not over. It is currently the war of longest continuous duration in the world.

Keeping Score

The following websites provide information on how to keep score of a baseball game:

http://ldt.stanford.edu/ldt1999/Students/dkerby/
  ldtportfolio/scoring/titlepage.htm

A fun site with a tutorial that includes quizzes to help you along.

http://www.baseballscorecard.com/kscore.htm

A good site for beginners, with the basics clearly explained.

http://people.iarc.uaf.edu/~cswingle/baseball/
  tutorial.phtml

This site includes a bibliography of books about scoring.

http://mlb.mlb.com/mlb/official_info/baseball_basics
  /keeping_score.jsp

The official site of major league baseball; however, the information on keeping score is minimal.

	1	2	3	4	5
Stanky 2B	7 B2FBFBF		5-4-3 BB		
Dark SS	5			4 BF	5 2BF
Mueller RF	7 2FBB			3! BB	FB
Irvin LF		6-3		5-3 B2B	
Lockman 1B		1Bx / 1B			6-3 2B2
Thomson 3B		x B / 7-6-3! 1B			x / 2B
Mays CF		7 B2			K BFF
Westrum C			1-6 3B 2FBBB		BBB IBB
Maglie P			5-4-3 FC 1-6 2BF		6-3
Rigney (for Westrum)					
Thompson (for Maglie)					
Jansen P					
Noble C					
Hartung (PR for Mueller)					
	0 / 0	0 / 2	0 / 0	0 / 0	0 / 1

1 LOB   2 LOB